# WHAT'S COME OVER HER

# WHAT'S COME OVER HER

HELEN MOURRE

*thistledown press*

National Library of Canada Cataloguing in Publication Data

Mourre, Helen, 1949-
What's come over her / Helen Mourre.

ISBN 1-894345-61-4

I. Title.
PS8576.O973W42 2003     C813'.54     C2003-911114-8


Cover photograph by David Mendelsohn/Masterfile
Cover and book design by J. Forrie
Typeset by Thistledown Press Ltd.
Printed and bound in Canada


Thistledown Press Ltd.
633 Main Street
Saskatoon, Saskatchewan, S7H 0J8
www.thistledown.sk.ca


Thistledown Press gratefully acknowledges the financial assistance of
the Canada Council for the Arts, the Saskatchewan Arts Board, and
the Government of Canada through the Book Publishing Industry
Development Program for its publishing program.

# ACKNOWLEDGEMENTS

I am grateful to the Saskatchewan Writers Guild Artists/Writers Colony at St. Peter's, Muenster where much of the writing for this manuscript was first conceived. Thanks also to members of the Rosetown Writers' Group and the Beechy Writers for generous critiques of many of these stories.

David Carpenter was a sensitive, wise, and skillful editor. My thanks.

Lynda Monahan and Sharon McFarlane were mentors and friends who saw me through the writing.

Thank-you to Dave Redell and Kelly-Jo Burke, producers at CBC radio, who brought several of these stories to life: "Coming Home", "Pilgrimage in Winter" and "What's Come Over Her". The story, "What's Come Over Her", was published in *Room of One's Own* and also on their web site.

And finally, thanks to my family for caring about what I create. My gratitude to Denise for her honesty and insight, and Michael & Danny for their computer savvy.

# CONTENTS

*For my family*

# Plagues

It was Saturday and hot hot hot. Ruth washed the kitchen floor and then dumped the pail of dirty water in the planters scattered about the deck; they were filled with shabby petunias and dusty miller and lobelia. She avoided looking at the rest of the farmyard where the grass appeared to have lost heart, having dried up and bleached to the colour of burlap sacking, and the leaves of the poplar and even caragana trees hung pale and limp. They hadn't had a lick of rain for two months.

She could get away with the planters only because she used recycled water from washing the dishes or the kitchen floor. The shallow wells and dugouts and sloughs had evaporated in the July heat wave. The water table was so low, in fact, that Rich had suggested they ration the house water, not a popular concept with a couple of teenagers who were obsessed with hygiene. No more twenty-minute showers for Megan who didn't seem to care if anyone else in the family had enough hot water to bathe with. More than once Rich had to go down to the cellar and turn off the hot water tap so she would evacuate the bathroom.

Megan and Chris were gone today with a group of friends, down at the river, swimming. It was so low this year, there were lots of little sand bars where they could sunbathe and shallow pockets of water to swim in. She worried about them all the time they were gone, though. Megan especially, her first born. She was too pretty for her own good. The delicate yet well-toned body on the doorstep to womanhood, the blond hair thick as a bumper crop of wheat. Add to that the pouty lips and an air of danger that the boys especially found attractive. But Chris, her younger brother, could be counted on to look out for her. She worried about him, too; it was hard to be a good kid.

The deck was on the east side of the house and already at two o'clock in the afternoon it was blessedly in the shade. She eased herself into an old canvas lawn chair and stretched out her too-pale legs. You could tell at a glance that she hadn't holidayed this summer. She looked like a sickly milkmaid. Besides, with no grass to cut and a scanty garden with few weeds she had little reason to be out in the sun. It must be thirty-five degrees today. Too hot to do anything even though the list of to-do jobs was playing in her head like a bad piece of music: Iron Rich's shirt for church tomorrow. Wash and chop the rhubarb. Start the potato salad for supper. But the choking heat and the dry air made her sleepy and lethargic. She could hear the steady whir of grasshoppers as they moved in from the west devouring her garden even as she sat there, but there wasn't much she could do about it. Rich was out this afternoon spraying edges of fields trying to keep the hoppers in control. Why did disasters come in clusters? First the drought, then the grasshopper plague. What was next? Was someone trying to make them leave here? She scanned the horizon. There had been an exodus: lots of her neighbours had packed up and left for the city, the Promised Land. She shuddered: fast-food franchises, apartment slums, noise pollution, obnoxious neighbours breathing down your neck.

The heat wave was good for tourism, at least; she listened to the traffic on the highway a mile to the north, camper trailers and half-tons pulling motorboats, heading east to Lake Diefenbaker or down to the South Saskatchewan River. A woman could go crazy here, she thought, just listening to the indifferent traffic speeding past, filled with holidayers desperately seeking a good time, the droning of grasshoppers as they advanced further into the yard, the hot wind blowing the papery poplar leaves. She watched a spider build a web in the corner of the house where the porch latched on to the roof. Why were the spiders so big this year? She shivered and looked away. Normally, the hoppers didn't bother the flowers on the deck but this year they were hungry. "Get," she said. "Get." She flicked them off the pink petunias even though it gave her the creeps to touch them; they had already chewed big holes in the leaves. The other day in the strawberry patch she'd seen a monster grasshopper. Rich didn't believe her when she'd told him. "I swear it was six inches long," she said. "Sounds like a locust to me," he said, "and I don't think there's any locusts in North America. I think they're in Africa and South America. But, I could be wrong." As far as she knew, a locust was just a king-size grasshopper, only more voracious. She wondered now if she'd only imagined it.

The sun had lost none of its heat; it shone stubbornly, sucking out what little moisture was left in the fields and gardens. Ruth's eyelids were growing heavy when she heard Max, their big chocolate lab, begin to bark. A vehicle was coming from the north, slowly; she could tell it was going to turn in. Realized it was too late to escape into the house. Who could possibly be visiting today? She didn't recognize the car, an older model four-door Chev that nevertheless was in vintage condition. The car was two-tone brown and tan, nicely colour coordinated with the drab landscape. Ruth counted four people in the car, two in the front and two in the back. She assumed they weren't salesmen; they usually travelled solo.

A woman and a young man got out of the back seat of the car. The woman was middle-aged and wore a flowered shirtwaist dress in shades of washed out pinks and mauves under a tired navy blazer. She had on pantyhose and plain black shoes with sensible heels. Just looking at her made Ruth feel even hotter. The man was much younger than the woman, in his late twenties perhaps. He wore wrinkled grey dress pants and a navy suit coat that almost matched the woman's. Dust had settled on top of his black shoes, in the seams. Barking with excitement, Max escorted them to the steps that led to the deck. They seemed to have no fear of the dog, scarcely gave it a second glance. Each of them was carrying books and pamphlets.

Ruth heaved herself out of the lawn chair and went towards them. "Hello," she said. "Can I help you?"

They ignored her question and smiled relentlessly. "Is it hot enough for you?" asked the young man. He had big teeth that were crowded together in a disorganized fashion.

Ruth wiped her sweaty palms on her denim shorts and lifted her bangs off her forehead. "Yes," she said. "It is hot."

The man and the woman kept on smiling as if they'd been programmed. The woman had a strange complexion, like uncooked pastry.

Ruth didn't offer any small talk to help them along. They were silent for a minute. Then the woman motioned to Max whom she'd ignored until now. "That's quite a welcoming committee you have there," she said.

That's why people have pets, thought Ruth, so when they don't know what to say to each other, they can always talk about their animals. "Yes," she agreed. "He's a bit of a show-off."

Max was beside himself, making frantic circles and whipping his long tail in erratic arcs.

"Okay, Max. Go and lie under the deck. Give us a break," Ruth said.

The dog looked ashamed. He put his tail between his legs and skittered away.

"What pretty flowers," the woman said.

"They're hardly pretty. They're practically dead. You know with the drought and everything," Ruth said.

"Yes," said the man, "I see you've got grasshoppers, too. These are terrible times, don't you agree?"

What was coming? What horrible prediction? Now. Here it was.

"Ma'am," said the man. He stroked his tie as if he were grooming a pet. It was the ugliest tie Ruth had ever seen. Violent swirls of psychedelic purple and scarlet. "Ma'am," he said again. Louder. More forceful. "Would you agree that the Kingdom of God is close at hand, that the end of time is drawing near?"

"No, I would not agree." Ruth brushed away a fly from her sweaty face.

The woman stepped up onto the deck. Ruth was close enough to her that she could have pushed her off the steps, but she resisted the temptation. The woman's eyes sent a chill through Ruth; they were blank somehow, but the set of her shoulders was unyielding.

She looked directly into Ruth's eyes. "At the end of time, God will send seven angels who will bring forth seven plagues, like the Egyptian plagues in the Old Testament. Those who worship false Gods will be afflicted with boils, the sea will turn to blood, there will be intense heat and drought and violent earthquakes and thunderstorms."

Ruth couldn't stop herself from smiling. "So what you're saying is this drought and grasshopper infestation is just the beginning of the end?" She placed her hands on her hips as if to punctuate what she was saying.

"Yes, ma'am. That's what I'm saying," said the young man. He was no longer smiling. "Now, ma'am, we don't mean to go getting anyone all upset. We just mean to tell you to be ready when the time comes."

Ruth laughed. "We've had droughts and grasshopper plagues here ever since people settled in this land. You folks have heard of the Dirty Thirties, haven't you? Our people lived through that. We'll survive this."

"Ma'am," said the woman, "there are signs all around you. We beg you to pay attention." She handed Ruth several pamphlets. Ruth glanced at the titles and tucked them under her arm.

"Thanks for stopping," Ruth said. "You might just as well go back the way you came. No one else lives up this road anymore."

She could see the two people left in the car had rolled down the windows and were fanning themselves. At least their bloody pamphlets were good for something. The man and the woman turned in unison and walked quickly back to their car as if they were glad to be on their way. The poor beggars. What a way to spend a Saturday afternoon.

She watched them pull out of the yard, their going raising little clouds of dust that hung suspended in the dry, still air. Ruth could hear the car turn onto the highway where it mixed in with the big trucks and the camper trailers. She could hear Max panting under the deck; he'd lost interest in the visitors as soon as he realized they were harmless. Ruth sighed and turned away. She stuffed the pamphlets in the tin garbage container at the corner of the deck. If only they weren't always so bloody sure of themselves.

*Ruth didn't want to think about predictions or religion or the fact that thousands of miles from where she had just stood on the deck in her farmyard and dismissed her zealous callers out of hand, in the flood plains between humid mountain ranges and dry plains, on the shores of rivers and lakes and seas bordered by arid regions, hordes of migratory locusts have been gathering for days. They are attracted by the ubiquitous moisture, but when the water dries up and the food becomes scarce they become concentrated in ever smaller areas. The crowding agitates the insects until the disturbance reaches a level that produces the swarming phase. Having a tendency for imitation, the entire horde begins to advance on foot as though under the influence of a mass psychosis. When the temperature is right they take to the air. Rivers are no obstacle, nor are cliffs or huge chasms as they ride the wind north. For days at a time they darken the sky and come to earth in the evening when the temperature drops, covering everything with a crawling layer. They are vandals of the worst kind: where they touch down nothing remains, not even the bark of trees.*

Lying next to Rich in bed that night, the blankets and sheets kicked off and the fan turned on high, Ruth tried to tell him about the company she had that afternoon.

"You should have been here," she said. She rolled on her side and rested her head on his shoulder. He gave off a strange odour, a mixture of sweat, dust and machinery oil, not altogether unpleasant.

"Why's that?" he said.

"Well, you always have more patience with that kind of thing than I do."

"It has to do with being open to other people's opinions."

"Yeah, I guess you're right. I was kind of rude. It just all seemed too melodramatic. As if they could predict the end of the world. As if anybody really knows. Except God."

She moved to her side of the bed. Usually, she and Rich curled up together like two spoons but tonight was too hot to cuddle.

"Don't worry about it, Ruth," his tone implying he had enough things to worry about.

"They talked about plagues at the end of the world like the Egyptian plagues. I guess if you add it up, we've had three so far this year, if you count the hailstorm that took out the north quarter. There were ten plagues in all, weren't there? The Egyptian plagues, I mean."

"I remember the last one for sure," said Rich. "The death of the first-born."

Ruth seemed not to have heard him. "I hope those kids get home pretty soon. It's getting late."

The bedroom windows were opened as wide as they could possibly be, but it seemed eerily quiet, as if the entire world was holding its breath.

"Why is it so quiet this summer?" she asked him.

"Because there's no water around to attract the frogs and all those other noisy creatures."

In the distance they could hear a car on the highway slow and turn onto the dirt road.

Ruth sighed.

"Must be the kids." She checked the clock radio. Twelve forty-five. Way past their curfew. She didn't feel like getting up and making a big deal of it, though.

As if he could read her thoughts, he said, "Go to sleep, Ruth. We'll deal with it in the morning."

\*\*\*

Ruth sat in the hard pew, fanning her hymnbook over her face. The church smelled of old wood and furniture polish, stale dust. She surveyed the straggle of people who had showed up for the Sunday service. A collection of white-haired widows and a few middle-aged couples like themselves, the high-school music teacher and the man who ran the hardware store. The minister, a woman from across the river, came every two weeks in the summer to hold a service. It seemed like it was expecting a lot to have her make all those miles when so few cared enough to show up. Maybe it was time to shut it down, Ruth thought. All the same, she drew strength from being here, from sighing her prayers along with her neighbours, from singing the simple hymns. Ruth had a strong, sure, soprano voice and as long as it wasn't too early in the morning, she could hold her own:

> *Amazing grace how sweet the sound*
> *That saved a wretch like me,*

*I once was lost, but now am found,*
*Was blind but now I see.*

Ruth wanted to believe that grace could make you suddenly see. She wondered if the visitors she had yesterday thought of grace at all. Did they credit grace for their one-dimensional vision? She didn't know.

*Through many dangers, toils and snares*
*I have already come.*
*Tis grace has brought me safe thus far*
*And grace will lead me home.*

She mentally ticked off the dangers, toils and snares in her own life: the drought and the grasshopper blight, the hailstorm, a rebellious teenage daughter. Could she count on grace to lead her home? She wasn't sure. Suddenly Rich tugged at her blouse. "Sit down." He motioned to the front where the minister was installed at the lectern getting ready to deliver the sermon. Ruth hadn't realized her mind was tangled up in runaway thoughts. "You okay?" Rich asked. He covered her small calloused hand with his big one. It was rough as sandpaper. The air in the church was lifeless and stale. Ruth could feel her cheap polyester blouse sticking to her back and her feet slipping in her sandals. She felt faint.

"I'm going to the bathroom," she whispered.

Even though there was a drought, the basement was damp and mouldy; it smelled like the inside of a refrigerator. Ruth creaked open the door to the women's washroom. Everything had shifted down here and it took quite a good shove to get it open. Once inside, Ruth leaned against the little white sink and felt its coolness through her cotton skirt. She thought she'd splash water on her face. Maybe that would startle her back to reality. But when she turned on the corroded tap, she was alarmed to see a horrible reddish coloured liquid come shooting out. She drew in her breath fast. Then quickly shut off the tap. Somehow, rust must have gotten into the water system. She'd have to mention it to Rich; he was on the maintenance committee. She felt as limp as a rag doll. She decided to wait for Rich out on the front steps.

\*\*\*

In the half-ton going home after church, the windows were rolled down letting in the hot, dust-filled air.

"You're sure the water was rusty?" He cranked his head to look at the field of stunted wheat they were passing. "That's funny, Ruth, because when I went down there to check it out, it ran clear as holy water."

It wasn't that he didn't believe her, it was just that it did not fit his logical mind. Here it comes, thought Ruth.

"Maybe you just should have run it a little longer. You know, flushed out the lines. It's been a spell since anyone turned on the water in the church, I expect. Probably been the first time this summer."

"Well," said Ruth, "it's never happened before that I can recall." She pulled her arm from the window where grasshopper missiles were bombarding it every few seconds. They could hardly see out of the windshield, littered with gory remains.

"You shouldn't let things get to you, Ruth," he said without so much as glancing her way. "Just one minute. I'm going to stop and see if I got those hoppers I was spraying yesterday."

He geared down and pulled into an approach. "I'll just be a minute." His tie blowing in the breeze like a windsock, Rich shouldered into the wind, checking for dead bodies. Ruth watched him and smiled; even though he was a big man with sloping shoulders, he still looked boyish. A farm boy's body that wasn't exactly athletic, but one that he could still count on to get the job done. Ruth opened the door to let more air pass through, but the heat assaulted her. She listened to the wind caught in the brome grass, bending it almost to the ground, and then lifting it back up, making a sound like loneliness, if loneliness had a sound.

\*\*\*

Back at the farm, Ruth busied herself getting some lunch on the table. Megan was up, still in her pajama pants and a sloppy T-shirt. She banged the cupboard door shut.

"Ah, Mom, didn't you buy cereal yet?" she asked.

"No, I haven't been to town for a while."

"There's never anything to eat in this house," she said sullenly.

"Well," said Ruth, "we're having some left-over vegetable beef soup and ham sandwiches. Care to join us?" She set four places on the table.

"Puke," said Megan. "I'll just have some cottage cheese." She took a plastic container from the fridge and starting spooning it into her mouth.

"Megan," said Ruth. "How many times do I have to tell you not to eat from the containers? Put some on a plate."

"But I'm the only one who eats the stuff," she protested.

Ruth stopped in her tracks and looked at Megan. There was something different about her this morning. As if she had discovered some new power. She looked again more sharply this time. Megan sauntered over to the kitchen table and straddled a chair backwards. There was something so suggestive in the movement that Ruth had to look away. Was it possible that her little girl had crossed the line into womanhood? Somehow Ruth knew what the answer was; it was something women could tell about one another.

Rich had his face buried in the *Western Producer* classifieds. He avoided confrontations.

"Where's Chris?" asked Ruth.

"Darren and Sean picked him up this morning after you went to church. I think they were going fishing." Megan tossed the empty cottage cheese container in the sink along with the spoon.

"Is he coming home for supper?" asked Ruth.

"I don't know. I'm not his mother," said Megan.

Rich dropped the paper and looked at his daughter. "What's with you, girl? Why are you so ornery all of a sudden?"

"Don't call me girl," she hissed.

Rich spread out his hands, palms up, and shrugged at Ruth.

\*\*\*

Coffee Row at Wing's Cafe. The women shoved two Formica tables together so they could better pool gossip and what passed for information gleaned from early morning talk shows on radio and afternoon television.

"How's everybody's garden holding up?" Ruth asked. They were on the far side of August now, and still no rain.

"Why bother about it?" said Aggie, a thin rod of a woman with leathery skin. "I can get all I need from the Hutterites up the road. They're all fixed up to irrigate. Why would I kill myself trying?"

"I agree," said little Mrs. Petrie. She had a halo of white hair and penetrating blue eyes. "Don't know why just because you live on a farm people think you have to have a garden. I quit growin' one the spring Alf died. Ground like cement and me hardly able to stand upright." She was referring to the big hump on her back from osteoporosis.

Laurene sat at the end of the table bouncing a baby on her lap. Ruth didn't know her very well. She'd married Cliff Chalmers a spell back, just about the only eligible bachelor left in the area. She was a city girl. The other women looked her way.

"Well, I had a good garden until two days ago. Then these big grasshoppers about six inches long moved in and cleaned the whole thing up. Cliff couldn't believe it." She tried to give the baby a sip of water from a teaspoon, but he twisted his face away.

The women looked at one another doubtfully. Grasshoppers six inches long? Ruth didn't dare mention she thought she'd seen one too about a month ago. She took a sip of coffee.

"They made a clean sweep," said Laurene. "Anything green and growing was just gone." She didn't seem terribly upset about her devastated garden.

She laughed. "They saved me a lot of work, I guess. Won't have to stand slaving over a hot stove pickling and preserving. Gee, I would have liked some fresh corn, though. It was just about ready to eat, but they stripped the cobs bare."

"Are they still in the yard?" asked Ruth.

"Well no," said Laurene. "They didn't stay long. Just long enough to wreck everything. Cliff was real mad. They even ate the bark off his precious apple trees. He spent all summer watering those things from the dugout. But I guess that's what happens here, eh?"

The women stared at her blankly.

Susie, the Chinese woman, who owned the cafe with her husband Peter, made another round with the coffee pot and the conversation veered off in a different direction.

"Did you hear about the young Larson boy?" asked Aggie. "His family farms that land just past the correction line." She looked down at her cup. Her timing was right on, thought Ruth. She knew just how to pause in the right spot to create the desired dramatic effect.

"No, I didn't hear a thing about it," said Mrs. Petrie. Her sly old eyes bored holes into Aggie.

Mrs. Petrie took a huge breath. "Well," she said, "he passed away night before last. Some strange viral flu, they think. He had a severe headache and by the time they brought him to the hospital and got the doctor from across the river, he was . . . " She paused.

"Oh no, that's terrible," said Ruth. "I hadn't heard a thing about it. "She wondered if Megan and Chris knew about it. They'd gone camping with friends down at the river last night.

All the women at the table made comments of shock or disbelief or sympathy. They drank more coffee. Talk turned to the age of the boy. Ruth thought he might even be the same age as Megan but she wasn't sure.

"He was the oldest boy in the family," said Mrs. Petrie, with authority. "The only boy, if I'm not mistaken." She pressed her tongue against the top of her mouth and then released it quickly. It was code for "What a horrible thing to happen but I'm sure glad it didn't happen to me."

Ruth got up. She threw a loonie on the table and pushed back her chair. "Let me know about the funeral arrangements."

\*\*\*

Ruth slid behind the wheel of the half-ton. Her hands were shaking. She gripped the wheel hard. Until it hurt. She felt the fear, like a small electric shock in her chest and then it settled down on her, solid and real. She cranked the truck left at the end of Main Street and headed east, not home but down to the river. She was crying. She knew she was probably the last person her kids wanted to see right now, but she didn't care. She would gather them up, her children. She would hold them safely in her arms. She would never let go.

## What's Come Over Her

Enid stands at the kitchen counter and rifles through the mail, looking for the June bank statement. She has to find it before Dutch gets home. SaskTel, SaskPower, bills from the chemical dealer, flyers from Pro-Hardware and the Co-op. Finally, at the bottom of the pile she comes across the envelope from the Royal Bank. She grabs the paring knife from the cutlery drawer and slits it open. Flips through the cheques until she comes to the one made out to Lorraine's Ladies Wear. One hundred and ten dollars. She's never in twenty-seven years on the farm spent that much on a piece of clothing. She feels her face go hot and then a trickle of moisture slides down her forehead and settles under her glasses making them slip down a notch. With clammy fingers, she studies the cheque. She hesitates for a moment, then rips it into quarters. Puts it in the garbage under the sink. Pushes it deep into the refuse. A slimy mixture of coffee grounds, potato peelings, burnt toast and soggy paper towels. She'll have to remember to take it out to the burning barrel before Dutch gets home.

Enid fills her lungs with air and the menacing fumes of Lysol. She'd given the kitchen floor an all-out scrubbing yesterday. Breathe in. Breathe out. She gives her shoulders a defiant little hitch and then heads out to the deck, flops down on the canvas lawn chair and stares straight into the sun. She can't believe what's come over her this last year. Her obsession with how she looks, what she wears. The dress was an impulse purchase one day three weeks ago. Enid had gone to town to pick up tractor repairs for Dutch. Then she'd stopped at the Co-op Service Station out on the highway to get gas. She'd forgotten to fill up at the bulk tank on the farm.

Dice Evans filled her car, washed down her windows and stopped to chat. Dice was compact and coiled, his skin-tight jeans showing off his well-toned legs. Enid could not stop staring. Until she noticed the hand with the missing thumb, and then she looked away too quickly. She hoped Dice hadn't noticed. She remembered he'd come back to town this spring from working on the oil rigs in northern Alberta. That was where he'd lost his thumb, she'd heard. Occasionally, he drove the bulk fuel truck out to the farm when the deliveryman was on holidays. Dice had moved back in with his mother after the accident, although Enid thought she'd heard about some woman he'd left back in Alberta.

"Is Dutch all finished seeding out there?" Dice said after he had filled her car. His voice was smooth as cream. He pulled the squeegee across the windshield in three easy swipes. Enid watched, fascinated by his graceful movements. The mutilated hand gave her the creeps, the way the thumb was so completely and neatly sheared off.

"We finished on Sunday," said Enid. "Now, we're praying for rain. As usual." She scanned the sky for clouds, but it was a blank slate.

"Supposed to rain tomorrow. But I wouldn't bet on it," said Dice. He wore sunglasses, the metallic kind that reflected everything back in miniature. They made her uneasy. Gave him some kind of advantage, she thought. He moved to the driver's side and cleaned both windows as well as the mirror. Enid noticed he paid attention to details. She liked that.

When he finished, he plopped the squeegee in the water bucket and looked at her for maybe a second longer than was necessary. Enid blushed and looked away." Do either of the boys farm with you now?" he asked. "I've forgotten."

"Nobody stays any more," said Enid flatly. "No, I'm afraid it's just Dutch and me."

"That's a shame," said Dice. "They ought to be there. To help you out."

"That's just the way it is," said Enid. "They have to make a living, too. Not enough money in this game any more for us to live. Let alone the boys and their wives."

Dice pulled the hose out of the car and turned to Enid. "You want to pay for this or just put it on the tab? I'll be delivering some to the farm one of these days. Dutch phoned about a fill."

Enid wondered why he was trying to help her out by not making her ask for credit. If it had been one of the younger guys pumping gas, they'd have made her pay cash on the spot.

"Sure," she said. "Just put it on the bill." It was easy to say, if you said it fast like that.

Dice's eyes dropped for a second before he raised his head and smiled. "See you out at the farm one of these days soon. Tell Dutch not to get his shirt in a knot. We'll have his fuel out there pretty quick. Oh, just a minute. Don't move." He reached across and plucked a white ball of poplar pollen from her hair. He flicked it into the air. "You take care now, you hear?"

"Thanks," said Enid. She snatched at her hair in a nervous kind of way. She felt a strange mixture of relief and shame and something else that she couldn't put a name to. When she got back in the car, her hands on the steering wheel were sweating. She wiped them, one after the other, on her shorts and then pressed her palms to her hot face.

After she'd gotten groceries at the ShopRite, she drove up Main Street and saw the dresses on display in the window of Lorraine's Ladies Wear and the sign, New for Spring. She had no idea why she suddenly angle-parked on the half-deserted street and went in. She hadn't been in the store for years. Wasn't even sure who it was that owned it anymore. Some divorced woman, she thought. The dresses hanging in the window were beautiful, all pastels. Creamy yellow, pale watercolour blue, and celery green. She thought back to the time she'd worked at the dry-cleaner in town that summer before she'd married Dutch. How she'd drooled over Miss Arsenault's couturier dresses. Enid stood for a long time just looking until a voice from the back startled her. "May I be of help?" A cultured, carefully restrained voice. Soothing.

Enid looked up. The woman was perched on a high stool behind the counter. Her dyed blond hair was sprayed into position and she wore a thick layer of make-up so heavy Enid suspected her wrinkles had all been filled in. "No, no thank-you," said Enid. She looked down at her faded navy shorts, her plain white T-shirt, her tired sandals. Then she looked again at the dresses in the window. She made a decision. "I'd like to try that one. The yellow one."

"What size do you take?" asked the saleswoman. "About a twelve?"

Enid looked down at her widening hips. "I used to take a ten."

The saleswoman assessed her. "This line of dresses fits on the small side." She hung the dress in the changing room with a clang.

Enid stripped down to her bra and panties and tried to avoid her reflection in the full-length mirror. Since her fifty-first birthday, Enid had noticed some drastic changes. She'd always prided herself on being in good shape, but now she was alarmed to see stretches of cellulite on her upper legs, a bulging stomach, and just enough pockets of fat here and there to give her whole body a lumpy, uncertain contour. She quickly pulled the dress over her head and twisted her arm behind her back and did up the zipper.

She looked straight into the mirror. Met her image face-to-face. The dress flattered her, a graceful A-line with enough excess material to camouflage the mysterious swellings. She fingered the fabric, a wonderful soft rayon with just the hint of a sheen as if sunlight had been trapped there. She twirled around, stood on tiptoes to get the proper effect. She pushed her grey streaked hair behind her ears, fluffed up her too-long bangs. She decided she must have it. Quickly, before she could change her mind. She pulled her shorts and T-shirt back on and took the dress out to the counter to pay for it.

"How did you make out, dear?" the saleswoman asked. "You didn't come out and show me."

Enid was anxious now to make the purchase and get out of the store. She had no idea what had come over her. Her hands shook so badly she could scarcely make out the cheque. She had to write it twice. The saleswoman wrapped the dress carefully in white paper and fastened a shiny gold sticker where the two edges overlapped. Enid wished she would hurry. She felt sick.

"There you go, dear. I hope you enjoy your dress." The saleswoman handed her a brilliant pink plastic bag with Lorraine's Ladies Wear embossed in gold letters.

Enid fled the store, pointed the '84 Pontiac towards home and drove without seeing, past the new green fields of wheat, past Ferguson's Seed Cleaning plant, past the Hutterite colony, past the McLean place with the red-and-white barn, past the dug-out where little Tommy Kennedy drowned.

When she got home, she hung the dress at the very back of her closet. Behind the dress she had worn to the boys' weddings and their graduations and her parents' anniversary. Then she made herself a cup of tea. Very strong.

***

After a while, Enid gets up from the deck and goes to the garden where she begins weeding. She picks cockle and portulaca and redroot pigweed from the rows of radish and lettuce and beets. She didn't even want to plant a garden this spring, but Dutch had insisted. A farm without a garden? What kind of farm wife was she, anyway? Most of her neighbours don't plant gardens anymore. It's less bother to buy fresh vegetables at the Hutterite colony up the road. It's easy for her neighbours, Enid thinks. They're not married to Dutch.

She stoops and picks. Straightens. Massages her aching back as best she can. This kind of work never bothered Enid until this year. She is surprised, really, by the violent onslaught of middle age. She had expected the deterioration to be more gradual. She envies Dutch, the way he appears to sail through everything with just as much energy as a thirty-year-old.

The sun rides high, so strong it almost bleaches out the blue of the sky. A flock of magpies circles above, biding their time to come and plunder the lettuce and the beets. Bully birds. They'll be fooled this morning, though. Enid has pounded stakes into the ground on either side of the tender plants and then wound strong black string from one stake to the other. When the birds fly into the string, their wings get caught, they panic, and then escape.

The heady smell of lilacs wafts over the garden patch. Enid decides to pick a bouquet for the table. She can hear Missy barking a welcome and Dutch's service truck roaring up the road. She jumps at the sound of it. She snaps off two more blossoms and hurries to the house. Dutch is in the bathroom off the kitchen, washing up. She can hear him splashing and snorting like an old elephant. The bathroom usually looks like a herd of them had a water fight when Dutch is through. Enid wonders if she's the only farmwife who has to wash the soap before using it.

"Dinner ready?" he yells.

Thank God for leftovers. Enid dumps a Tupperware container of vegetable stew into a corning-ware dish and pops it into the microwave. She's failed badly at house-training Dutch. If she weren't around, he'd starve to death.

Dutch yanks out a chair and seats himself at the kitchen table. He flips through the morning mail which Enid has left lying there. Scatters it in all directions. She stands at the counter breaking lettuce into a bowl for salad. Holds her breath.

"Here's the goddamn bank statement," says Dutch. "How bad is it?"

"Well," she hesitates. "It's not as bad as I thought."

31

"Christ," he says. "Where does all the money go?" He quickly flips through the cancelled cheques. His fingers, thick like sausages, travel down the list of numbers until he comes to the bottom line.

Enid slices tomatoes and cucumber to garnish the salad. Her hands are shaking. The heavy-sweet smell of the lilacs makes her nauseous. Suddenly, the knife veers off to the side shearing a small piece of flesh from the tender end of her middle finger. Blood spatters over the white cutting board like graffiti.

"Damn." She runs cold water over her finger and quickly grabs a bandage from the kitchen cupboard.

"What happened, Enid? You hurt yourself?" He doesn't look up when he says this, continues flipping through the cancelled cheques until he's satisfied. Enid sets the stew and salad on the table. Dutch helps himself and then mixes everything together on his plate so that it resembles nothing like the original.

She stares at the jam jar of crocuses; she remembers that time one spring when he'd brought her a bouquet of crocuses from the south pasture, how shy he'd been when he'd given them to her, how her pleased reaction had somehow made him feel foolish. There was just that one time she can remember.

A fly circles Enid's head erratically. *ZZZzzzZZzzzzZ*. Swoops past her ear and then lands on the table a few inches from Dutch's plate. She fetches the fly swatter from the nail that holds the calendar. *ZZZzzzZZzzzzZ*. Enid brings the swatter back to her shoulder and tries to anticipate where the fly is going to land. She slaps the swatter down — whack — on the table, making Dutch's cutlery spin.

"Christ, Enid, do you have to swat flies over my food?"

Enid hangs the swatter back up on the nail. Sits down at the table. Dishes up a plate of stew and salad. The fly is crazy now. ZZzzZzzzzzzZZZZ. Making irregular loops over the table and then bombarding the window, trying to escape. She hears the buzz inside her head as if the fly is trapped in there, trying to get out. "What's wrong?" he says. "You haven't said a word since I got home. You get the weather forecast?"

Enid pushes the stew and salad around on her plate. "No, no," she says. "I've been out in the garden all morning. Weeding."

"Well, I've got work to do. Gotta finish that summer fallowing. Won't be back 'til late. Don't wait on supper for me." He throws the cutlery on his plate. She hears the screen door slam and the pointy hook latch fly up and ping against the doorjamb and she knows he is gone. The buzzing in her head stops.

***

It is hot. Enid sits on the couch and watches the afternoon soaps. Then Oprah. If only she knew as much as Oprah. Oprah would know how to cope with middle age, with a sagging body, an atrophied mind, inertia. *O praise be to the Goddess Oprah.* Enid pays attention to herself as she breathes in and out. Watches the rise and fall of her chest. After a while, she hears a vehicle coming up the drive. She sits up at once, startled, because it couldn't be Dutch home so soon. He's summer-fallowing the south quarter and won't be back 'til late. She listens to the sound of gravel crunch all the way up the driveway and then fade away. Whoever it is, isn't planning to come to the house. Curious now, she eases herself off the couch and goes to the kitchen, lifts the curtain and peers out. The Co-op fuel truck is backed up and a long hose, like an umbilical cord, is connected to the big silver fuel tank. Light explodes off the tank.

Enid can't see which deliveryman it is. She can only see his legs as he walks behind the truck. Her heart begins to pound and her fingers run through her hair, lifting it, and she whispers, "Jesus", wondering how bad she looks.

She hears the roar of the delivery truck as it pulls away from the tanks. It comes to a stop at the back door and Enid listens to the truck door slam. She goes to the screen door and peers through. Dice Evans jumps out of the truck and starts towards the house, the yellow sale bill fluttering in his hand. Enid steps out onto the deck and smoothes her cotton blouse over her hips. Pushes her glasses up on her nose, fingers her left ear lobe as if looking for something there.

"Hi, Enid," he says. He moves easily, as if indifferent to gravity. Not like Dutch who seems to attack the very earth he steps on. Sometimes, Enid expects little bits of the earth's crust to come flying off when he passes by.

"Dice," she says. It's not her voice she hears but a small choking sound that seems to come from some distant place.

"Here's the bill of sale, Enid." He hands her the thin yellow slip of paper smudged in one corner with a greasy thumbprint.

"Thanks." She looks down at the bill and begins to stroke the corner with her thumb.

He stares across the yard. "You do all the yard work here, Enid? It looks real nice."

Her hands flutter to her hair. She leans against the screen door and feels the sticky dampness of her blouse against her skin. She shivers.

"Would you like to come in for a cool drink?" she says.

He hesitates. "I suppose I could. Don't have another delivery until tomorrow. Wouldn't want to get back to town too soon or the boss'll just give me more jobs."

"Come in," she says, holding the screen door open. "Seat yourself."

She fetches the iced tea from the fridge.

Dice takes off his metallic sunglasses. Puts them in the pocket of his tan work shirt. When she lifts her head to meet his gaze, she finds herself staring into his dark eyes.

"It's real homey in here, Enid. You do the decoratin'?" He motions to the wallpaper, cheery yellow and white gingham with a border of sunflowers.

"Yes," she says. "Thanks." She isn't used to men noticing her efforts. She had the kitchen wallpapered a week before Dutch even made a comment. She tries hard to keep the place up even though there's scant resources to do it with. She hopes Dice doesn't notice the holes in the worn-out linoleum.

She turns her back to him to get the glasses from the cupboard. Then pours iced tea and ice cubes, her hands shaking so bad she overshoots the glass and spills a brown puddle on the kitchen table.

"Damn," she mutters under her breath. She grabs the dishcloth and sops it up, rinses it under the tap and wipes the Formica table again.

"Hey," Dice says. "What you so nervous about? Slow down, girl." He lays his crippled hand on her bare arm, forcing her to sit.

Her eyes avoid his hand even though disturbing images of it caught in the rigging chain flash before her. She wonders what it would feel like running up her thighs, the inside of her legs.

Dice's laugh startles her. "Go ahead, Enid. Why don't you ask me about my hand?"

She jerks her head up, surprised. "No . . . I . . . I . . . didn't mean to . . . no . . . I don't."

He rocks back on the wooden chair, his feet coiled around the rungs, his balance perfect. "Workin' on the rigs is a dangerous business, Enid. You gotta know when to get in the clear. Before you get hurt, that is. It's a fine line." He takes a swallow of iced tea and rocks back on his chair again.

"I learned my lesson the hard way." The front legs of the chair connect with the floor. Slam.

"Enid, I've got something to ask. I've been meanin' to for a long time, but I just haven't got around to it."

Enid fingers the small gold chain around her throat that she never takes off. She laughs nervously. "Of course, Dice. Ask away."

Dice coughs. "Folks in town tell me that good lookin' brunette that works at the Royal Bank is your cousin. Is that true?"

Enid hesitates. "Yes. Yes, she is. Just moved here from up north. Why did you want to know?"

"Well, I'd like to ask her out. I was wondrin' if you could introduce us sometime. I'd sure appreciate it."

She sees colours and shapes colliding, like a child's angry painting. And then an emptiness as if a vacuum has sucked out all her oxygen.

"Sure," she says flatly. "I don't mind. Anytime."

Dice pushes the crumpled yellow sale bill lying on the table towards her and shoves his chair back. "Gotta go now, Enid. You take care now, you hear?"

"Sure. Of course." She doesn't get up to see him out. Bastard, she thinks.

She sits at the table and hears the sound of the truck fade into the distance. *You gotta know when to get in the clear. Before you get hurt, that is. It's a fine line.* She gets up from the table. She watches herself pick up the empty glasses and place them in the dishwasher. She watches herself wipe the kitchen table. And wipe it again. Then she watches herself go to the closet, take out the yellow dress. She fingers the fabric lovingly. She thinks about taking it back and getting her money, but the anger she feels at this moment demands something more.

Instead, she carries it to the burning barrel, douses it with gas, and sets it ablaze. It is surprising how quickly it burns. How quietly. A late afternoon wind picks up the stray ashes which are as thin as parchment and carries them over the caragana hedge into the green fields of wheat.

## Swimming into Light

They had decided to canoe across the lake from where they were staying at Kapasiwin Bungalows to the main beach area. Enid had never canoed before, scarcely knew which end of the boat was front or back. She didn't let on to Dutch even though she knew he didn't have much experience with canoes either. Other than the time he'd made love to her in the bottom of one at Jackfish Lake the summer they were nineteen. She can't imagine doing anything so ridiculous now. Later on, they had a motorboat when the boys were both at home; they water-skied and went fishing. But now it was just the two of them.

"You may as well sit in the back, Enid," said Dutch. He tossed her a life jacket.

At first Enid thought this odd, that Dutch would ask her to sit in the stern. She knew just enough about canoeing to realize that the person sitting in the back had control over where it went. But Dutch had hurt his back just before coming to the lake, moving an antique piano out from the wall so she could houseclean. She felt partially responsible for his injury.

Enid pushed her arms into the clumsy life jacket, zipped it up, and tied the cords at the bottom securely together. She took off her sandals and stepped into the lake, the icy water sending needles of cold up the calves of her legs. She inched her way along the gravelly bottom and climbed in awkwardly.

Dutch rolled up his pant legs, removed his socks and shoes and threw them into the bottom of the boat along with his life jacket. He handed Enid a paddle. She looked at it like it was some sort of strange apparatus that had nothing to do with her; she felt hopelessly inept and clumsy.

"It's a paddle, Enid," said Dutch. "It makes the canoe move forward when pulled through the water. Like this." He demonstrated in an exaggerated, mocking kind of way.

After finally settling in, they managed to maneuver the canoe away from the shore and point it towards the main beach area. It looked about a mile away. She dipped her paddle, first one side and then the other. She could hardly believe the resistance of the water. She could feel her arm muscles pulling and her back tightening up.

"We're going crooked," yelled Dutch from the front. "Better straighten her out or we're going to end up in the middle of the lake." Dutch was a natural athlete; everything came easy to him. He did it all: the slow-pitch team in summer, old-timer's hockey in winter, and golf whenever there wasn't snow on the ground.

Behind his back she mouthed his words. Damn it, she thought. Can't he see I'm trying? She paddled fiercely on the right side of the canoe trying to align it with the shoreline.

She wondered how deep the lake was here; she stuck her paddle vertically in the water and was surprised to find it didn't touch bottom. She thought about telling Dutch. Decided negative. The plan had been to stay close to shore in case they capsized. But as usual he was in charge of the operation. Better not burst his little bubble.

It was a glorious day, the sky a pure azure blue with just a few wispy rags of clouds. Stands of dark green spruce, almost black, made a jagged line along the edge of the lake. There was silence between them: she heard the liquid sound of the paddles as they connected with the water, the whoosh of the boat as it pulled forward. Overhead, sand hill cranes and swallows flashed against the sun. Such a glorious day and yet she felt a huge emptiness inside. Part of it she knew was the kids. Their leaving and how she was suddenly flung back on herself. They'd put their oldest son on the plane for Australia last Monday; he was married and living there now. A tall, gentle giant who loved to cook and garden and read books. The one who always remembered to put something in her Christmas stocking. She hadn't dared go into his room when they'd gotten home from the airport. Instead, she'd madly housecleaned the office, pitching out old magazines and papers, washing walls and light fixtures and book shelves. "What's got into you? Why are you crying?" asked Dutch on his way out to the shop. He didn't put much stock in emotions.

She rested her paddle for a minute, peered over the side of the boat into the dark water. The reflection gave nothing away, like her reflection in the mirror in the morning. Disconnection. Who was the woman staring back at her? Enid didn't know anymore. Ahead of them, motorboats and seadoos crisscrossed, making waves; they looked threatening. She hoped they could keep the canoe out of their path. She could tell they were drifting farther out, though. She paddled only on the right for a few minutes, but the canoe seemed to have a life of its own.

She thought about going for a swim. Later in the afternoon, maybe, when it warmed up. Sometimes the cold water could shock you into feeling something. She'd learned to swim in this lake the year she'd turned nine. She could still remember that summer.

Lessons at eight o'clock in the morning: five pathetic little figures stood shivering on the edge of the dock. As a joke, they had called their instructor Algae (behind her back, at least), a big-boned girl with skin the colour of toasted marshmallows. She blew her lifeguard's whistle and assembled them together in a little huddle, gave instructions on the particular stroke they were learning, and then told them to jump into the water. Cold turkey. Every summer for six years, Enid and her sister took swimming lessons on the money their mother made from cleaning other people's houses. They wouldn't have dared refuse. Enid had almost drowned when she was a kid, before the time of the swimming lessons. Her mother had come to the lake with all five kids by herself; she had relatives who lived close by. Naturally, Dad didn't come because there was too much work down at the hardware store. One day, as the story was told and re-told, Mother and her younger sister, Shirley, had all five children down at the beach, the two girls and their older brothers. Five kids under the age of six. Suddenly, Shirley yelled, "Enid's gone under! Enid's gone under!" Her mother walked right into the lake with all her clothes on and plucked her out of the water, gasping and spitting. Enid has no recollection of this event other than through her mother's telling of it. Right then and there her mother decided that some day her girls would have swimming lessons. It wasn't clear why Enid's brothers were left out. They were older of course, and being boys, they could always be counted on to fend for themselves.

The swimming pool one summer. That's where she'd met Dutch. The summer she was eighteen, the summer she worked at the dry-cleaner. It's funny that she'd met him at the swimming pool because Dutch didn't swim, just about the only sport he didn't do. He used to come to the pool to check out the female lifeguards. Roaring up in his '55 red-and-white Monarch, spitting gravel, the radio blasting Patsy Cline or Elvis. And then he'd just sit in his car and stare at her, cocky as only an eighteen-year-old can be. Enid got the idea that there was nothing wasted on Dutch. His body was small and efficient, densely packed. And in thirty years not much had changed. His hair had turned an attractive pewter-grey and there was less of it. He'd developed a little paunch that conveniently disappeared in the summer when the farm work started up again.

"Hey, Enid, paddle hard on the right," said Dutch over his shoulder. "We're going to end up on Dead Man's Island if we're not careful." He sounded pissed off at Enid, as if he thought she wasn't pulling her weight. Damn you, anyway, she thought. Okay, if that's how he was going to be, she'd quit paddling altogether. She took her paddle out of the water and rested. It wasn't long before Dutch yelled again, "Okay, Enid. Give 'er."

She bent forward in the canoe and tried to get a rhythm going. Maybe it was like swimming, she thought. Maybe, out of the blue, you just got it. The summer she was nine came back to her as if she was paging through an old photo album.

Algae standing on the dock, the morning sun forming a glow around her golden body: Enid, the idea is to pull yourself through the water as smoothly as you can. You're not mixing a cake. Demonstration from Algae with arms above her head. Look at your sister. She knows how to do it.

And then, suddenly, Enid got it. Bent arms catching the water just at head-level, curled fingers cupping, arms pulling while the legs alternately churned back and forth. Head in; exhale. Head out; inhale. She opened her eyes under the water. Except for the roaring in her ears, she was fascinated by this other world. She watched a little school of minnows swimming carelessly along the bottom. She saw a beer bottle and a large rock with pink and black sparkles.

"Enid . . . Enid." Dutch's voice broke through, like static ruining her favorite hit-parade song. "It's getting kind of choppy here." He motioned to all the water-skiers and seadoos. "We better move out to smoother waters."

She wondered how they were supposed to do that. It seemed as if they'd been swarmed by every kind of speedboat. Those little seadoos were the worst: noisy, aggressive little machines. There should be a law against them. She glanced around at the approaching wake from the speeding boats and realized they were in trouble; even Enid could see. She looked to Dutch for her cue.

It was hard even to talk anymore; the noise of the motorboats was deafening. Dutch waved his paddle in the vague direction of an open expanse of water that seemed to be clear. Enid dipped her paddle and steered to the left. At last they were turned and heading back to Kapasiwin. Thank goodness, she thought, as she watched the distance between them and the other boats increase. She was getting too old for all this excitement.

"Make her work. Make her work," shouted Dutch. Enid had a sudden vision of Dutch as a Roman soldier barking orders at the galley slaves in *Ben Hur*.

Now, she realized she'd misjudged the distance. They'd probably paddled two miles instead of one. And they had to go all the way back. Her biceps felt like elastic bands stretched to their limit, and little trickles of sweat ran down between her breasts.

"Keep her moving. Keep her moving, Enid." The galley boss had spoken yet again. She could feel a little pulse of hatred beating against her temple.

Ahead of them the lake had become choppy, the wind having sprung up from somewhere, the way it did here. A seadoer out of nowhere suddenly made some annoying figure eights right in front of them, and then took off to harass someone else.

Enid thought she was going to pass out from the heat. She couldn't remember why she decided to stand up in the canoe to take off her bunny-hug. But she did remember Dutch yelling at her, "Christ, woman. You're going to tip the canoe. Sit down. Sit down." She'd turned to glare at Dutch just as a huge speedboat flew past creating a monster wave. Suddenly, she lost her balance and plunged head first into the lake, the roar in her ears and the brutal slap of the water confusing her for a moment. And then the whole damn canoe flipped over.

The water so cold, Enid wanted to cry out. She looked around for Dutch. At first she couldn't see him so she swam around to the other side of the canoe. There he was, just surfacing about ten yards from her. She was shocked to see the look on his face: the anger replaced by raw fear. He was thrashing wildly with his hands, but no sound was coming out of his mouth. It just kept opening and closing, like a dying pickerel. Where was his life jacket? She spun around in a circle, treading water, looking. Nothing. It must have caught under the seat somehow. She didn't know if she was strong enough to swim him into shore; they'd drifted out quite far now. And getting the canoe flipped back was probably too hard for her to do alone.

She looked around for a rescuer. All the boats seemed impossibly far away, even the speedboat that had just passed them. She waved her arms and yelled *help*, but it all seemed so pathetic. Then she made a decision. She'd have to try to swim him into shore. He'd gone under twice already.

She swam over and tried to get behind him so she could grab hold, but he lunged for her and dragged them both under. Enid kicked herself and Dutch to the surface and uncurled his fingers from around her neck. Then she pushed herself away from him.

She treaded water just out of his reach and began talking in a slow even voice. "It's me. Enid. You have to trust me; I need your help. I need you to be calm." His wild eyes reminded her of someone who had just walked into a dangerous jungle. She felt as if she was looking at a stranger. She could see him going under again. One of the paddles was floating about ten feet from her. Enid swam over and grabbed it. She held onto it like it was a club. Just before Dutch disappeared under the water again, she lifted the paddle and brought it down hard on the top of his head. He went limp immediately, and she caught him behind the shoulders. He was lighter than she imagined. She began kicking into shore, moving slowly, a few feet at a time. Big breath — fill the lungs with oxygen. Kick. Repeat. Her mind and body totally focused on what she had to do. Her waterlogged blue jean cut-offs were a handicap, so she pulled them down over her hips and kicked them off. There, that was better. She was glad she couldn't see Dutch's face; she just knew it was out of the water and with any luck he was still breathing. The crown of his bleeding head dug into her breastbone until she wanted to scream. She looked up at the indifferent clouds so far away, saw the shoreline coming closer and closer. Saw the little cabins clustered along the edge of the water take shape, the blobs of colour evolve into separate boats anchored at the edge of the lake.

Just when she felt as if she couldn't kick her legs one more time, she discovered the sandy bottom. When she stood up the lakebed seemed to be shifting and her feet had trouble finding purchase, but she dragged Dutch up onto the beach and collapsed. She felt as if she might pass out herself until she heard him begin to cough and vomit beside her. He was going to be all right.

***

Dutch was pretty quiet the rest of the holiday; he sat reading in his lawn chair and looking out across the lake as if he was in a trance. Not once did he even acknowledge that Enid had saved his life.

They left for home two days before schedule. Enid drove. They were passing the Emma Lake turn-off when he turned to her and said evenly, "Why did you do it, Enid? Why did you stand up in the boat?"

She didn't answer. She took her eyes from the road for a second to look at him. He had a white bandage turbaned around his head and part of it covered his left eye that she'd managed to graze with the paddle when she'd knocked him out. With the dressing hiding his eye that way, it was as if he couldn't see her. She turned away and looked out the window at the sunny fields of canola, the placid cows grazing in the green pastures. The highway stretched before them, wavy with heat and humidity. She felt as if she was swimming, alone in a long narrow tunnel. She imagined herself nine-years-old again, strong and proud that she'd learned to do this new thing. At the far end was a circle of bright sky, a fierce blue. It was painful to look at, but she swam towards it with all her strength.

## Putting Words To That Summer

I was eighteen that summer, the one before the rest of my life was to begin. My brain had been clogged with algebra equations, French verbs and Shakespeare, but all that was about to change: my dad had gotten me a job at Fenwick's Dry Cleaners. My friends worked at Wing's Cafe waiting on tables or at the Co-op filling shelves or packing groceries. When the summer was over, I'd be heading off to university, on a scholarship, the first one in our family of five to go "away" to school. I couldn't wait to leave Glendale and get on with my life. I was determined not to follow my older sister who had bogged down in our little town, was married with four busy pre-schoolers who sucked up all her energy.

Fenwick's Dry Cleaners was a low insulbrick building that slouched at the end of Main Street. A chute connected the storefront business to a small shed at the back where the dry cleaning took place. I'd been told the clothes were shipped back and forth in this chute. It all seemed very mysterious to me. Was I the only one who thought the clothes were magically cleaned by air?

When I went to see about the job, Mother insisted I wear a prim white blouse (the one with the Peter Pan collar) and my navy pleated skirt. Looking at myself in the mirror that morning, I seemed a little too anxious to please. I arrived at the appointed hour at Fenwick's Dry Cleaners and asked the gypsy-like woman at the desk for Mr. Fenwick. A strong odour of solvent permeated the air; I could already feel the heat of the day starting to build. I looked about the small reception area: a plain wooden counter, waist-high, ran the length of the store and behind it on two levels hung little clusters of clothes, each little group in its own plastic baggie. It all looked so orderly and strangely satisfying.

Mr. Fenwick (Junior) finally emerged from the back. A large man, loosely built, with a blank face and eyes that resembled my aging dog King. He looked nervous and in a hurry. He said he was glad I'd stopped by; my dad had told him I might like a job for the summer. It looked like good old Dad had already done the groundwork. This was going to be easier than I thought. I told him I was going to university this fall and I could sure use the money (I figured it wouldn't hurt to play up the struggling student image a bit).

He said I could start right away. I'd be working from nine until five, Monday to Friday and the odd Saturday. He nodded to the dark woman who had stood staring at me while I was talking to Mr. Fenwick. I found out later her name was Kathleen. The name didn't seem to match the way she looked, which was very exotic. Her face was long and angular. I wouldn't have called it beautiful in the Hollywood sense, but her skin had a mysterious luster that suggested the tropics. My mother and her friends complained bitterly about the dry prairie air, how it sucked every last bit of moisture from their skin. Kathleen appeared to have no such problems. Her not-quite black hair was held up with two combs covered with jade and ruby coloured gems. I was fascinated.

She told me I'd be looking after customers at the front as well as other chores at the back when I had the time. She gave the impression that she was the one who ran the place. She looked like she'd done a lot of hard work in her life, a lot of lifting and carrying, but when she spoke her speech was amazingly cultured. Kathleen answering the telephone: *No, Mr. Fenwick is unavailable at this time. Perhaps you could call later?* Her voice rising at the end of her sentence to imply a question, when we all knew it wasn't really a question. Everyone in the place deferred to her, from Mr. Fenwick, to chubby Mrs. Williams, who sat at the sewing machine off the main reception area and did alterations, to Reg, Kathleen's scrawny little husband, who operated the steam press.

Did I only imagine she resented me? In any case, she was not forthcoming about what my chores were. Mrs. Williams had pity on me as I stood helplessly behind the desk and waited on my first customer.

"Here, Enid. Now you stamp the same number on the bill as well as the little white tag with these metal claws that you attach to the clothes. Then when you do mark-up, you match the numbers on the tags to the bill." She wheezed her way back to the sewing table.

It seemed easy enough. I soon learned the hardest part about working at Fenwick's Dry Cleaners was suffering the heat that built up from the two steam presses at the back, but I got used to feeling sweaty and light-headed. Whenever I looked at the clock, it was always disappointing. I came to view Fenwick's as a kind of purgatory. I was sure it was the closest I would ever get to the kind of hell that Sister Mary Thomas told us about in grade four Catechism.

I caught on to the job quickly. Exchanging pleasantries with the customers when they entered (the mandatory remark about the weather), fetching the little plastic baggies of clothes and writing out their orders. The better the description on the order form, the easier it was to match when doing mark-up: one ladies Audrey Hepburn style wheat coloured linen sheath dress with matching belt, one ladies white box-pleated skirt with dropped waistline, one two-piece Clarke Gable double-breasted pinstripe suit. I tried to imagine what they would look like when they were put on the bodies of the people that owned them. I began to see clothes in a new way, as obscuring things underneath or possibly transforming them. I was always astonished when Mr. Beaton from the butcher shop at the corner of Main Street and Third Avenue (the largest man I'd ever seen) showed up with his trousers to be cleaned. He would always lumber in with this slightly ashamed look on his face. I tried to be as discreet as possible when writing out the slip, knowing that when Reg got the pants on his steam press he would have a hay-day. Reg, who was a little bony guy, could afford to ridicule. "I wonder where he got these made up — at "Tent and Awning Supply?" And yet, when I saw Mr. Beaton wearing the pants, they didn't look as big as when they were draped over the metal hanger with no frame to flesh them out.

I used to love it when Miss Arsenault, the French teacher at the high school, would bring in her wardrobe. I was fascinated by the couturier labels, the fine fabrics, wools and linens and shantung, the way the garments draped, the attention to detail that set them apart from the usual run-of-the-mill clothing that came into the shop. My own mother favored flowered housedresses and on Sundays, the same two-piece navy suit she had thrown together on her Singer sewing machine.

I came to enjoy working in that purgatory — the camaraderie, the good-natured joking. Reg was always trying to fix me up with someone. "Hey, Enid . . . I've got a nephew working on the oil rigs. He's going to be home this weekend. How about I fix you up?"

"No, that's okay," I'd say. Really, me go out with a roughneck? I'd heard some stories about those guys. They were out for one thing. I was going to wait until I got to university this fall where I was sure there was a huge crop of eager, sensitive young men just waiting to be tapped. The girls I hung around with agreed on one thing. You could like boys . . . but not too much.

One day I'd heard on the radio that it was going to be a scorcher — a high of ninety-eight degrees, the announcer said. I decided to live dangerously and wear my little plaid halter-top with a white blouse over it. I thought I could get away with not buttoning the blouse. I'd just finished waiting on my first customer, Mrs. Elliot, the Anglican Church minister's wife, a stern, forbidding looking lady. She called me "dearie" and didn't mention my halter-top at all. Well, I thought, if it doesn't bother Mrs. Elliot, then I guess I shouldn't have to worry.

Mrs. Williams was placidly hemming trousers at the sewing table; Reg was sipping his cup of instant coffee when Kathleen called me over. I will never forget it. As she talked in a low, neutral voice about what was left at the back to mark up, she calmly buttoned my blouse from bottom to top without missing a beat. I was pretty careful about what I wore to work after that. It was obvious that Kathleen belonged to the camp of people who thought clothes should obscure what was underneath.

One day I was left to mind the shop at noon hour. I'd just finished ironing a dream of a dress, a full-skirted peach taffeta with a plunging neckline. I held it up against me and drooled. What event in Glendale could you wear this lovely creation to? I couldn't think of one. I found myself dancing along the workroom floor holding the dress in place at my waist while I swirled and looped my way between the racks of clothes, until I ran headlong into Kathleen who was standing in the doorway to the workroom.

"Go and hang that dress up," she said. I couldn't read her face. Was it anger, disgust, disappointment? I did what I was told. I felt like a little kid getting caught playing dress-up in her mother's clothes.

I wanted to understand how this woman, who led the most ordinary of lives, could command such deference, such respect, such authority. Where did it come from and how did one go about getting it? Reg and Kathleen were wonderful together. He often called her darling. I had never heard a man use a term of endearment like that before and I was amazed at its power. My parents never called each other anything but "Mom" or "Dad" as if in those two titles their whole lives were marked out. Sometimes when Kathleen would be sitting at the sewing table doing books (it seemed everyone gathered at the sewing table), Reg would set a cup of instant coffee beside her in silence, like an offering. There seemed to be this unspoken agreement between them. Perhaps Reg would forever be the gift-bearer, and Kathleen would always be the recipient. I was too young then to know about the politics of a relationship.

Reg and Kathleen had no children, a fact that caused endless amounts of speculation in our small town. My, my . . . tut, tutted my mother and her friends. What a shame. They wondered endlessly who was to blame. Was it her? Or maybe he'd been hurt in the war? Reg had been in the Italian campaign and apparently that's where he met Kathleen. I couldn't see what the big deal was with having children. As far as I could tell, it had made my parents anxious and burdened down by responsibilities. Sometimes, I preferred to forget that I owed my existence to them.

I used to spy on Reg and Kathleen when I walked downtown on Saturdays. There was a small patio behind their house made of cement blocks. You could just catch a glimpse of it through the caraganas. Here, the two of them sat in their lawn chairs. Music came from somewhere — maybe a radio or a record player. I'd never heard anything like it. It sounded like an opera of some kind but I didn't know anything about Classical music. I could only guess at the emotion it conveyed for them. When I walked down the street, it made me want to cry, as the notes rose and hung there in the dusty hot afternoon. I thought of the white sacks on wheels that Reg pushed endlessly back and forth in the humid workroom and Kathleen bent over the ironing board straightening the cloth with one hand and pushing and pulling the iron with the other. This music seemed to lift them out of their drab, daily lives and make them somehow glamorous. As I walked up the street, a fierce longing came over me, a desire to have a piece of that other world. I was almost sure that going away to university that fall would be the beginning of a new life. After spying on Reg and Kathleen, I would meet my friends at Reynold's Hardware. We'd spend all afternoon listening to forty-fives played on Mr. Harrison's little portable record player in the sound booth at the back. Occasionally, we ended up buying one or two. "Calendar Girl" or "Walkin' With My Angel" or "Ten Lonely Guys".

Sometimes, if it was hot, we'd go to the swimming pool. Most of the guys our age liked to show off, wrestling with each other in the water, pushing each other in. Driving the lifeguards crazy. There was one guy that used to come in his car to just watch us girls. Dutch Munroe from south of town. You could tell he thought he was pretty good looking by the way he slouched against his car in his tight blue jeans and skimpy white T-shirt. He didn't mix with the other guys. Maybe because he was older, but I guessed he was checking us out. Once I caught him looking at me as he leaned against the hood of his '55 Monarch. I had to look away before he did.

\*\*\*

I'd been working at the dry cleaners about a month when Mr. Fenwick came to see me. Would I be able to take Kathleen's place for a few weeks? Could I manage the front as well as doing mark-up at the back? This request coming from Mr. Fenwick in his quivery anxious voice made me feel like a soldier being asked to report to the front lines.

I was already rising to the top. My dad would be so proud. I managed the next few weeks with no major disasters. Well, there was almost one. A young man who worked in the Royal Bank was getting married and had brought his suit in to be cleaned. This was all fine and good until I came to do mark-up and alas . . . there were no pants to be found. Had they mistakenly got put in with someone else's order? The day grew closer and closer to the wedding. Mr. Fenwick was panic-stricken. He thought our reputation would be ruined. Finally, after phoning the young man to explain our predicament, Mr. Fenwick discovered the future groom had only brought in the suit coat to be cleaned. Of course, there was a general feeling of relief all around, except for me who had written up the bill. There was the evidence for everyone to see. It said, *one grey striped two-piece suit.* Somehow I knew that Kathleen would never have let something so silly happen. Whenever Reg looked at me after that he wore a little smirk that seemed to say, *You're not so smart after all.*

During the few weeks that Kathleen was gone, Reg was a changed man, like a planet torn from its orbit. Gone were the little jokes, the teasing. His face became drawn and colourless. I used to watch him at the steam press as he'd expertly slip the pants over the table and then with both feet bring his weight to bear on the pedal that controlled the steam while forcing the upper table down with both hands. He did all this without thinking, while he stared out the little two by two window across the street to where an empty lot played host to a disheartening crop of dandelion and pigweed. During this time Reg didn't even stop for his instant coffee break, preferring instead to see his shift straight through, as if it was some kind of restitution.

Mrs. Williams had filled me in on the reason for Kathleen's absence. Nobody at the shop wanted to talk much about it, especially with Reg working there, but the word was out that Kathleen had a rare form of leukemia — terminal. I didn't know how to respond to this news. Nobody close to me had ever died before or had a serious illness. I was shocked and saddened and also confused at the little stitch of satisfaction that had sewn itself into my brain and that I tried to suppress. I knew that a big piece of Reg's heart had been torn out of him. I wanted to go and put my arms around him as if that would take away his pain. I wanted to say something to him, something comforting, maybe something funny, but no one said anything, and it was almost as if Kathleen had been written out of our lives before she needed to be.

Summer was wearing thin. A couple of weeks before I left for university, I brought my own rather meager wardrobe in to be cleaned. I planned to iron the clothes myself and save the cost of a dry-cleaning bill. Kathleen had returned to work after her treatments, but already you could see that she was different. Not only in physical appearance — the loss of weight, the drawn face and sick colour but something else. It was hard to explain. It was as if she was living in a different dimension already, something almost spiritual although I knew Kathleen didn't go to church.

My last day of work I came in to find that Kathleen had pressed all my clothes, as only she could press them — to perfection. I felt guilty for my healthy body, for my life that stretched before me as full of possibilities as a summer sky.

When I went to thank Kathleen, I found her sitting at the sewing table hemming some trousers for Mrs. Williams. I didn't know how to begin.

"Ah . . . Kathleen . . . Thanks for pressing my clothes. You didn't have to do that, you know."

"Well, I hear you did a pretty good job filling in for me when I was away. I appreciate that," she said quietly.

"Oh . . . it was nothing." I stood twisting one of the metal hangers in my hands, not knowing where to look. I didn't know why thanking Kathleen should be such a hard thing to do.

"So, you're leaving town pretty soon, I hear. Going to school in the big city?" It seemed there was a hint of sarcasm in her voice that I hadn't heard before.

"Yes." I said. "I'll be taking an art's degree."

"You look like you're anxious to leave."

"I can't wait," I said. If the truth were told, as the time grew closer for my departure, I had moments of doubt, my stomach going all fluttery and nervous. But I figured once I got to university, I would settle in.

Without looking up, Kathleen poked her needle into the pair of men's pants she was hemming. "You'll never be able to leave this little town behind you, even though you might think you can," she said.

There was a space in the conversation. She waited for me to fill it. For the life of me, I couldn't think of one word to rub against another. And so I stood there in the claustrophobic sewing room with the sweat running down my underarms while Kathleen calmly hemmed trousers, making long arcs in the sultry air with her needle and thread. Even though she didn't say anything, I realized I'd been dismissed. I was never so glad to hear Reg's voice, "Got the kettle on for coffee break, Enid?"

The staff at Fenwick's Dry Cleaners gave me a leather briefcase as a going away present. They thought where I was heading, I'd have need of something like that. But I couldn't help noticing the small smile on Reg's face as he presented it to me, almost mockery. As if he knew something I didn't.

\*\*\*

I left in the fall for university. Being cloistered in a small room in the student residence suited me well. My own little desk and study lamp and narrow bed were all I required. I was here to do a job. There were expectations and I would try to live up to them. The routine was soothing and dignified: classes and term papers to write, special lectures and concerts to attend. No one pressing me to join the volleyball or basketball team. Walks with new friends in the bowl, a huge grassed area nestled between buildings and flanked by beds of flowers. Sometimes, by the lily pond, I shared a cigarette with a boy from History 101. The university buildings with their elegant gothic architecture, their imposing tall windows and turrets and spires were everything that Glendale was not. I had escaped.

Or had I?

Mother wrote newsy little letters informing me who'd had a new baby, who'd gotten married, and who'd died. It was through Mother that I found out about Kathleen, about her death. I wondered how Reg would survive. He would be like an asteroid, randomly travelling without a direction to follow. It made me stop and think about things like loneliness. That look I'd seen on Reg's face when he realized Kathleen wouldn't make it.

I tried to put words to that summer. For a moment the news of Kathleen's death made a small blip on the radar screen of my life. It took me out of myself and placed me in a world that all too soon I would be a part of. At the time, I could not have known that even as I resisted it, I was hurtling helplessly towards it.

# Circles

Clare had thought nothing of taking lunch out to Stormy in the field that day; he was swathing the hilly piece over by the Hutterite colony. The lunch wasn't anything special: leftover roast beef on home-made multi-grain bread, freshly baked in the bread machine that morning, some crumb cake and fruit, a thermos of coffee with too much sugar and enough milk to give it the cast of muddy slough water. She didn't know how he could drink the stuff. She had tried to get him to switch to decaff or at least to cut down on the sugar, but Stormy wouldn't heed any of that healthy-living propaganda. Clare knew he would do things his way until a crisis hit him head-on.

She loved this time of year on the farm, the almost-tropical sky enfolding the yellow fields of wheat. She had to stop for a minute to edit her thoughts. Come to think of it, there seemed to be a shortage of wheat fields this year. Now, they were surrounded by lentils and chickpeas and canola. Even canary seed. "Canary seed," Stormy snorted. "Bird feed. I'd rather feed people."

Stormy had been a holdout, refusing to grow the more profitable pulse crops that many of his neighbours were trying. The way Stormy figured it, you would just be farming for the chemical companies and the machinery dealerships, the new crops requiring multiple applications of designer chemicals for one disease or the other and fancy new headers and pick-ups to harvest them. At his age, he just couldn't see the sense in it. Clare agreed. As it was, they used enough chemicals on cereal crops for for various problems: weed control or grasshoppers or midge. Besides, they were on the verge of getting out of farming. Their son, Dean, was waiting on deck, willing to give up a good job in the city. Crazy kid.

The Hutterite colony was up ahead, the light reflecting off their shiny new buildings. A mile south, McLean's old red barn made a splash of colour on the faded landscape. Clare slowed for the approach to the field, turned off the dirt road and pulled to a stop a few yards in. It was an unwritten law that you didn't drive in a field that had been swathed. Grounds for divorce on some farms. She'd always been pretty careful since that time she'd driven into a field of durum and the catalytic converter set the dry stubble ablaze. Every fire truck in the municipality had shown up. Lots of excitement. Even made the front page of the *Rosetown Eagle*.

Clare killed the motor on the half-ton and leaned her head out the window, inhaling the dry grain smell. She stretched out her bare legs under the dash, and squinted into the field. She could make out Stormy's outfit just coming around the ravine, his red Massey '90 with the yellow umbrella pulling the matching red swather. She guessed it would take him about ten minutes to reach her. She loved the lay of the land here on this quarter, the way the little ravine curved its way through the gentle hills. She had often thought that it would have been a nice place to build a house. The swaths formed a symmetrical pattern, bending around the ravine in a convex shape and then gradually straightening out as the swather veered towards the edge of the field.

Across the road from where Clare had parked the truck lay the remains of an old pasture, owned and neglected by a couple of bachelor-farmers. The two old guys had landed in the old folk's home in Swift Current, and the rumour was circulating that the ambitious Forsyth brothers had bought up the half section where the pasture was to add to their empire. Up until last year, a pair of burrowing owls had been leasing the weedy patch of earth, but Clare had noticed on her last trip out to the field that they'd disappeared. She felt sad; she'd always enjoyed watching them hover and flap about. She'd have to ask Stormy about them.

She could hear the rumbling of the tractor and the clatter of the swather as Stormy steered the bulky equipment towards her. She waved and then watched him push in the clutch and throttle down, preparing to stop. Clare got out of the truck and walked around to the back, yanked open the end gate, slid the orange plastic cooler over and undid the lid. She could hear Stormy approaching through the stubble, breaking straw as he came, taking a giant step to clear each swath. In his army-green work shirt and matching pants, worn to a state of comfort, he was at ease in his own skin, and completely at home on the land.

He made himself comfortable on the end gate and grabbed a sandwich from the Tupperware container. "Jesus, Clare. I wish you'd quit makin' this damn brown bread."

She's wasn't about to repeat the litany of reasons that should've convinced him a long time ago it was good for him.

Stormy hung onto his coffee cup like it was a baseball and he was about to wing it to homebase. Suddenly, as if he'd just thought of something, he jerked his head up. "Hey, Clare, where's Moses? Didn't he wanta come?"

Moses was a big black and white dog of uncertain pedigree who'd been a gift to their son from an old girlfriend. The girlfriend was long gone, but the dog had stayed, a lopey creature that barked ferociously at anyone who came into the farmyard, unless there was someone at home and then he hid under the deck. He had an extravagant amount of energy that much of the time seemed to have no purpose other than to catapult him from one adventure to another: chasing cars up the gravel road, running after his ball, poking around in ditches after mysterious prey.

"No," said Clare. "No, I couldn't find him when I was ready to go. You know how he is, always off on an adventure." She took a sip from her bottle of water and munched on a piece of crumb cake.

Stormy helped himself to another sandwich, crumpled the wax paper into a ball and tossed it in the ditch. "There's sure a lot of straw in this field. The heads aren't that big, though. Just one more rain when they were filling would've made all the difference." He swirled his coffee around in his cup.

Clare reflected on how they seemed to alternate between boom and bust on the slimmest of variables. Not enough rain at the right time. Not enough heat when needed. Not enough days to ripen it.

"Sure does look pretty, though." Clare looked across to the ravine. She hopped up on the end gate and bit into an apple, the juice splattering her chin.

Stormy gave her face a swipe with the sleeve of his shirt. "You're droolin' there, Hon."

"Yeah, well, you've got a gob of mustard right there on the end of your nose." Clare took a paper towel and wiped at it, harder than she had to.

"Hey, enough of that now," said Stormy. He motioned towards the pasture across the road. "I wonder what happened to our burrowing owls. They still haven't come back."

"Yeah, I was just going to ask you about that. I think it's because there's not very many gophers anymore."

"What would that have to with it?" asked Stormy.

"Well, think about it. The owls make their nests in badger holes. The badgers prey on gophers. So, if there aren't any gophers, there aren't any badgers and there aren't any burrowing owls. Remember the food chain we learned about in grade eight science?"

"Grade eight? Hell, that's a lifetime ago." He drained his coffee cup and tossed it in the lunch box. "They'll always be gophers. I don't worry about that. Bloody nuisance, anyway."

"Come to think of it, when's the last time you heard a meadowlark? Or a song sparrow?" asked Clare.

"It's been a spell, I havta admit. What are you getting at anyway?"

"We're poisoning their habitats, that's what."

"Well, what d'ya want me to do? I'm a farmer. That's how I make a living. Hey, you wanta come for a ride with me after lunch? I'm gonna do the other side of the ravine. Maybe it'll be better. A little lower there. More moisture."

Clare realized there was no way she was going to win this one. Although Stormy was a moral man, he was also pragmatic. Like most farmers, he would deny any sentiment he might have for the land in favor of extracting the most resources from it.

"Sounds good to me." Clare wiggled her butt off the end-gate and started putting things back in the cooler. She wasn't especially anxious to get home where a huge batch of

64

cucumbers waited for pickling. She'd play hooky this afternoon.

\*\*\*

It was about two o'clock when they finished the north end of the field and moved across to the ravine. Coming down into that valley could take your breath away. The sight never disappointed her. But today was different. Even Stormy sucked in his breath and said quietly, "Jesus Murphy. What the hell?"

Down in the plateau maybe a quarter mile ahead, Clare could see the reason for Stormy's weird reaction. Three circles of various diameters lay etched in the field of wheat, placed precisely as plates on a table. Stormy pulled back on the throttle and stopped.

"Well, look at that. Clare, you don't have the camera in the truck, do you?" Stormy asked.

"Well, no," Clare said. "I didn't expect to see anything special today."

"Jesus Murphy," Stormy said again. He seemed to be in a trance. Suddenly, all his cockiness was gone.

He rarely asked Clare for advice, but now he said, "What do you suppose we should do?"

Clare hesitated. In spite of the warm day, she felt a chill run up the back of her legs. She'd read a little bit about crop circles. There were different theories about their origins: natural causes, flying saucers, pranksters.

"Well, let's just drive on down there and have a better look," said Clare.

"Why don't we leave the tractor here and walk down?" he asked.

Clare's T-shirt was sticking to her back when they finally reached the first of the circles. Hands on his hips, Stormy walked around the circle's perimeter, staring thoughtfully. The wheat was folded about an inch from the ground so that while the stalks lay flat in a swirled pattern, they were still not broken. A tail in the form of a cross protruded from the southwest quadrant of the circle. He bent down to examine the stalks of grain that had been flattened but not damaged. He toed the edge of the circle with his work boot.

Clare stepped off the perimeter. "I think it's about fifty feet," she said.

With outstretched arms, they swished their way through to the other circle on the east. "It looks like the cross design is exactly the same," said Clare. "The same size and everything. It's even pointing in the exact same direction. Amazing."

The last circle was located a bit west of the other two, a doughnut pattern, a ring within a ring. Clare was not surprised to see the tail again, the identical cross pattern pointing in a southwesterly direction.

They checked the field for signs of entry. There was no indication that anyone had entered from ground level. It looked to Clare as if whoever had created the circles must have accomplished it from above.

"You know a few nights ago, Clare, there was a big meteor shower. Do you suppose it could have been that?"

"Well, that might account for the big circles, but what about the crosses?"

"There's power lines and cellphone towers not too far away. It must be some kind of magnetism," Stormy said. He seemed more sure now. He could talk himself into anything if he talked long enough, the words once spoken aloud creating their own truth.

Clare was silent. She'd never seen anything like this before. What on earth could have made them?

"Come on, Clare. Don't suppose it's anything to be upset about. There's probably a damn good logical reason for them. Nothing to get all worked up about." Stormy was anxious to get back to work. He started up the hill without a backward glance. Clare hesitated. Then reluctantly she turned into the wheat field, pushing forward. Once in a while she shoulder-checked to see if the circles were still there.

***

The news about the crop circles spread as fast as chickenpox. Once Clare had spilled the beans on coffee row, there was no turning back. *The Western Producer* and the *Rosetown Eagle* both sent out reporters to get the lowdown. A vanload of Hutterites came and had a look. As a rule, you wouldn't find a Hutterite wandering around a swathed field in the middle of harvest when there was work to be done. Some guy from Alberta drove out, took pictures, some samples of grain and then left. A busload of kids from the local high school made a field trip one day. Clare was kept busy manning the phone that just about rang off the wall. Could she tell them how to get to the field? Did they have any idea what had caused them? Had they found any more circles?

Stormy had to post "No Trespassing" signs at the edge of the field. Most people were pretty respectful but some swaths had been crushed and mangled. He didn't want to spoil anyone's fun, but he'd have to pick up the swaths in the field pretty fast or the whole thing would be ruined. Clare was surprised that at least Stormy had taken the time to swath around the circles. The one thing Stormy didn't like, though, was his beautiful wheat field being turned into a circus and the curious tramping around on his property. Trespassing. Stormy didn't take kindly to trespassers. Years ago, when the natural gas pipeline had gone through the south quarter, he had threatened to blow them away with a shotgun.

Even with the excitement over the crop circles, harvesting had progressed well. The weather had been great, the combine had held together, and so far they were still talking to each other. The only field left to harvest was the one with the crop circles.

This morning, Stormy was anxious to get going, but heavy dew had delayed them. He was on his fourth cup of coffee — the bottom of the pot, industrial strength. He plopped his usual three spoons of sugar into the dark liquid and stirred vigorously.

Clare watched him and shook her head. She pulled the blind down a few more inches to screen out the sun exploding through the kitchen window.

"Do you know if McLeans are finished yet, Clare?"

"Harvesting? I don't know. With all that new equipment I suppose they are. Why?"

"Well, I think I'll get them over to clean up the circles with one of their fancy new headers. I don't have anything that'll get close enough to the ground."

Clare warmed her hands on the coffee mug. Quietly, she said, "Why do they have to be cleaned up anyway? Why can't they be left alone? They're not hurting anything, are they?"

"I just wanta get rid of them. That's all. No big deal."

"I didn't say it was a big deal. I just don't know what the rush is."

She pushed ahead. "You know, maybe it's time to stop asking what caused the circles and start asking why?"

"What do you mean?" he asked.

"Well . . . maybe someone is trying to tell us something."

"And that someone would be . . . ?" Stormy teased her.

Clare knew she was on shaky ground. She'd have to be careful how she phrased her next words or Stormy would just laugh at her. She looked out the window at Moses before she replied. He was begging at the window again, as if he was at a fast food drive-through. "Maybe . . . just maybe . . . we've been trying too long to control our environment. Look at the chemicals we pump into it year after year. We don't really know the long-term effects of what we're doing. Maybe we've used the land long enough. Maybe it's time to move on."

"Here we go again. Sounds like a bunch of New Age mother-earth bullshit to me," he said.

"Well, I don't know," she said. "I'm just saying . . . let's keep an open mind."

Stormy looked out the window. He offered by way of an answer, "Looks like the dew's gone. Come on, mother. Let's get goin'. Supposed to rain tomorrow."

\*\*\*

By the time the sun had crested the deep blue September sky, Stormy was back riding the combine. Clare had been promoted from cook to truck driver, as was usually the case whenever their son couldn't make it out from the city to help. She didn't mind, really. So far, she hadn't burnt the clutch out, or left the end-gate open, or sideswiped the combine when unloading. Stormy didn't trust her yet to drive the combine. It was on its last legs and had to have a lot of TLC to keep operating. She liked driving the truck and Moses had come along for company.

Clare had also brought a book to read. *Women are from Venus Men are from Mars*. Her neighbour up the road who had lent it to her, had highly recommended it. Clare didn't know what all the fuss was about. She'd always known men and women came from different planets. That was just plain old common sense. Between loads she read a few passages, skipping from chapter to chapter. When Stormy had seen her reading it, he'd growled, "Oh, so you're reading science fiction now?" Clare didn't bother explaining.

They'd been all afternoon on the north side of the field. Everything had been humming along, smooth as chokecherry syrup. The old combine was steadily devouring the swaths, round after round. Clare was keeping up, gathering the grain from the combine and then dumping it in the steel bin at the edge of the field. With any luck, by suppertime they would move across the ravine onto the south side. Where the crop circles were. If everything went well, they'd finish the field before midnight.

She yawned and leaned against the rear window of the truck. It had been a long day; she fantasized about a luxurious soak in a hot tub. Cool clean sheets. Moses was out chasing something that only he could see, thrashing through the swaths erratically. If only she had as much energy. She closed her eyes for what seemed like a minute. Suddenly, Stormy's raspy voice on the CB radio jolted her awake. "Clare, where in the hell are you? The hopper's full. Come and dump me, and then we'll stop for supper."

She coaxed the truck into life, called to Moses and began to head over to the combine that was finishing up the last swath. Good, thought Clare. That left the other side of the ravine for after supper. They should finish up tonight. Except for the crop circles.

\*\*\*

Clare was glad a full moon was riding low in the eastern sky, a huge disk of orange light. It served as a reference point, helping to keep her bearings. She knew how easy it was to get lost in the middle of a field at night, to mislay her sense of direction. It had happened a few years ago in this same field. The lights from neighbouring fields had suddenly all looked the same. She had panicked, driving off in every direction, not stopping to think, to reason it out. She had roared up to a set of combine lights, and then realized just in time the outfit wasn't theirs and took off again. The neighbouring combine operator must have wondered for a long time who the phantom truck driver was.

She hoped there would be enough room in the bin for all the wheat from this field. Otherwise, they'd have to stop and move the auger to another one a mile up the road. Not a job you'd want to tackle in the middle of the night. And knowing Stormy, he'd want to finish.

She'd have to talk to him again about the crop circles. See if she could persuade him not to do away with them. It didn't seem right somehow. The way she saw it, the circles were sacred. Destroying them would be like desecrating a holy cathedral.

Clare decided to let Moses out of the truck for a run. They were parked at the northeast corner of the field, the truck lights picking up the broad outlines of the circles. She was amazed that even with all the people tramping through the field, they were still perfect. Even the crosses were intact. Clare noticed how tonight they seemed to almost glow. She could see the combine lights maybe a quarter mile off to the west. In another ten minutes Stormy'd be here.

Moses was off in the ditch chasing who knew what. Clare called to him. "Moses. Come here, boy." Her voice sounded puny and uncertain. She shivered in her scanty T-shirt; she'd have to remember to bring warmer clothes to the field. "Moses," she called again. She could hear him coming now. From where he was in the ditch, he'd have to run through the crop circle to get to her. But then the strangest thing happened. Moses stopped dead when he got to the edge of the circle. Stopped and stared at the flattened wheat. Then he began to whimper, little bits of noise that seemed trapped inside his throat, as if he was too scared to let go of the sound. She tried calling him again. "Moses. Moses." Softer this time. She tried to keep the fear out of her own voice.

Suddenly, she knew what she had to do. Stormy could *not* combine the crop circles. She would not let him. It was as simple as that. She could see the lights of the combine coming at her. She had to have it out with him now. She ran towards the combine, waving her arms frantically over her head. Then she heard all the power systems on the combine wind down as if they were being sucked into a vacuum. It stopped barely two feet from the edge of the circle. Stormy opened the cab door and stepped onto the ladder. He turned and yelled across, "What the hell are you doing, woman? Have you taken leave of your senses?"

Moses began making laps around the crop circles, faster and faster. There was no stopping him now. Clare looked across the darkened land to where the neon-orange moon seemed to be rising . . . rising in the sky. Her head was spinning as she ran towards Stormy. When she got to the combine, he scrambled down the ladder and clutched her shoulders. "What's the matter, Clare?"

"Look at Moses. He won't enter the circles. He just runs around and around. He's so scared. You have to leave the circles alone, Stormy. Do you understand?"

She was yelling now and the sound of her voice surprised her. "Do you understand, damn it?"

Stormy let his big hands fall to his sides. "Moses," he called. "Come here, boy."

Moses stopped doing laps and loped over to him. He whimpered and nuzzled his big head into the man's leg. Stormy stroked the dog's head, trying to comfort him but the dog would not be calmed. Every time Stormy took a step towards the circle, Moses headed him off.

"What's the matter, boy?" asked Stormy. "You scared?" He looked at Clare.

She stood, embracing her body with her long pale arms, her face looking up with wonder at the orange moon that seemed to glare down on them. Stormy tracked her line of vision. Ghostly shreds of cloud passed in front of the moon and then disappeared leaving only its blank, dispassionate face.

# Coming Home

Marci's hiking boots bite into the hard-packed snow on Main Street. She loves walking here alone at night, gazing up at the stars. This little town, maybe fifty or sixty dwellings in all, feels like it's perched on the edge of the world. It's a startling clear night, the Milky Way tinseling the sky from one horizon to the other. If she's patient enough, she can begin to decode the constellations: Aqaurius, Leo Minor, Draco, Monoceros and Lacerta. This is one of the things her ex-husband had taught her. She remembers lying on a blanket in their backyard so they could look up at the entire sky. She sighs and shifts her curling broom and gym bag to her other shoulder.

Marci can't believe she got talked into adding her name to the curling list. It must be twenty years or more since she's curled. Back in high school, in Glendale, it was just about the only game in town. And still is. A game on ice where civilized people throw forty pound rocks up a slippery surface and somehow have expectations of preciseness. She's come back to her hometown to teach high school English. Starting over and running smack into middle age; divorced with grown kids. She should be home tonight marking midterms, a Romeo and Juliet assignment, but she thinks she'll throw up if she reads one more adolescent rant on unrequited love.

The rink marks the end of the street. An ugly, bunker-style building that adds nothing to the townscape. She nudges the door open with her shoulder and steps into the waiting room. A rush of warm air mixed with the smell of coffee and stale grease clashes with a moldy, wet-sock kind of odour. *This is what she's come back to.*

A few curlers have already gathered. Some are putting on their curling shoes while others lean leisurely on their push brooms. She recognizes a few of them. Blake Friesen. The same boyish face, a little heavier along the jaw-line and the thick head of hair now veined with grey. There's Carl Derocher. A good ole boy. Pulls beer for the under-age kids looking to get hammered on Friday night. Still shows up at the year-end grad parties even though he's gaining on forty-years-old. No one seems especially enthusiastic about being here. But neither do they seem to mind. They've showed up, they seem to be saying, as if that in itself is accomplishment enough. And maybe it is, Marci thinks.

She pulls off her winter hiking boots and bends to lace into a pair of old runners that have had other lives: early morning tramps through Kinsmen Park when she lived in the city, that last holiday with the kids, hiking at Jasper. She notices the other women have specially made curling shoes with fancy logos. A slider on one foot and a grip on the other. They all wear curling pants with a sporty stripe up the side. She's probably dressed all wrong: blue jeans and an old nylon parka with a small three-corner tear in the left sleeve. Jamie, an athletic looking woman who works at the drug store and teaches aerobics on the side, says to Marci, "You know, you're not going to be able to move in those things. Should've worn leggings or something that gives." Marci hates women like

Jamie. She watches her power-walk home from work every day, her arms swinging like an army recruit in basic training, her short little legs scissoring up the street. All motivation and muscle. Nothing flabby going on there.

"I guess you're right," says Marci. "I forgot. It's been so long since I curled." She looks down at her faded jeans, a no-name brand from the Saan Store.

"You'll be curling with us," sighs Jamie. "You can play lead." She adds. "If that's all right with you?"

"Great." Marci remembers this is where they put the greenhorns. If they make a mistake, there are still six rocks to correct it. She also recalls the leads have to do an awful lot of sweeping. Oh dear, this had seemed like a good idea at the time, when Doug Wiebe, the science teacher, had cornered her at the photocopier and encouraged her to sign up.

Their skip is a big bear of a man named Scotty. Marci's heard that Scotty likes to imbibe a few, especially when he's curling. The other player on their team is the school principal, Lew Bartock. He's new at the school this year, too. His wife teaches in another town about fifty miles away so Lew commutes every weekend.

"Glad you made it, Marci," says Lew. He's wearing sweat pants, the same grey ones he sometimes wears to school when he's instructing a phys.ed class. A black bunny-hug with a Garfield logo. Marci notices when he has his back turned to her, he has almost no bum, flat as the face of a cliff. For some reason she can't explain she finds this attractive. Lew has this quiet, self-assured way of speaking. "I suppose you're an old pro at curling. Most small town people are," he says.

Marci laughs. "It's been a while. Quite a while."

"I'm sure it'll come back to you quick enough. Kind of like riding a bicycle."

Marci's hoping she won't embarrass herself, especially in front of the school principal. She realizes she'll have to face him at school tomorrow and five days a week for the next seven months. Out on the ice both teams shake hands before starting. They say things like "good curling" and "good game". It's all so non-threatening, but still Marci has a hard little knot in the bottom of her stomach. Jamie does a few stretches on the ice before starting. Probably a good idea, Marci thinks, but she feels self-conscious. If she gets down there, will she make it back up? Since the onset of her forty-fifth birthday, she feels like her body is realigning itself, the load somehow being distributed in new and strange places. She sighs.

Lew is playing third so he gets the dubious honour of flipping the coin to see who throws the first rock. The rest of his job description includes holding the broom for the skip and marking up the score. In the hierarchy of curling, he's kind of like a vice-president. Lew pulls a dull looking nickel out of his pocket and seeks out the third of the opposing team, a large woman who wears an old-styled siwash sweater. Marci remembers her dad wearing one of those to the curling rink. Thumb ready to flip the coin Lew asks, "What'll it be?"

"Heads," she says.

Both thirds look down at the nickel as if they are looking for the winning number on the Lotto 649. Lew turns to Marci. "We lost the toss. Looks like we throw first." *Great*, Marci thinks. This gives the other team the advantage because they get to throw the last rock. The game is starting to come back to her. She had tried to get her ex-husband, Gerald, to curl with her but he was born and raised a city boy, didn't mind telling her he thought it was more boring than going to a tractor pull. He preferred a game of chess with one of his colleagues from the English department at the university. It seemed like such a small thing to get upset about. But it was the stockpiling of all the small annoyances over the years that eventually began to chafe at the tender underside of their relationship until it was raw.

Marci nudges one of the blue rocks with her foot, sliding it over to the hack. She has forgotten how heavy they are. She cautiously puts the toe of her right foot in position and bends both knees until she is squatting on the ice. She balances by holding onto the broom, lifts the rock, then pushes forward out of the hack, releasing the rock with a slight turn to the right. An in-turn. She feels like an old barge being pulled out of dry dock. Sluggish. Immediately Scotty yells at Lew and Jamie. "Sweep! Sweep!" They follow Marci's rock up the sheet of ice, gallantly pushing their brooms back and forth. Marci's rock dies just before the hog line.

"That's okay," says Jamie with a little smile. "The ice is usually pretty tough the first end." She swells with good will.

The next rock Marci throws seems to have a life of its own. It careens wildly into the boards before it reaches the house.

Once again, Jamie offers words of comfort. "Must have picked up something to set it off course," she says.

Marci mentally rolls her eyes. Even she can tell she missed the skip's broom by a mile. She can feel her heart thrashing erratically in her chest when she sweeps the rock up the ice. This can't be good for you, she thinks. All this frantic activity after being dormant for such a long time. Following the divorce, she'd settled into a long and crippling depression. It wasn't that the divorce had been a sudden thing; she'd seen it coming for years. But she wasn't prepared for the pain. She took a leave of absence from her job and cut out all physical activity. Gained twenty pounds and lost all her self-esteem. When a job came up in her old hometown, Marci had a sudden, inexplicable desire to move back, try to make a life for herself surrounded by friends and family. She had a brother living on the family farm, happily married with a bevy of kids. But even though he tried to include her, he had his own life to live. How much time did he really have to spare for his middle-aged sister whose life had become dismantled. Her mother was still living in town, but she too was busy with her bridge group, her church, her small clutch of friends. Sometimes Marci feels like a trespasser. And other things have changed since she left more than twenty-five years ago. A big Hutterite colony had bought out several farmers a few years back. Lots of families had packed up and moved to the city. The town had become a haven for people looking for a cheap place to live. Marci has no quarrel with these people. It's just different. She can't help feeling that she has more of a right to be here than they do.

It's her turn to throw again. She hopes she can find her weight and hit the broom at the same time, a feat that seems more and more impossible as the game progresses. So far she's missed just about all of her shots. Either they slide through the house or they stop a couple of inches before the hog line. The one rock she did get in, she took out again with her next one. Even after this happened, Scotty still didn't yell. "That's okay. That's okay," he kept saying. She can't help wondering how Gerald would have reacted. Not in any public way, of course. Oh no, he was too sly for that. She can't help remembering one night after they'd had another couple on the faculty over to play bridge. The woman was a snob, wrote book reviews for the local paper. Obviously, the assignment had gone to her head. Marci became distracted by the woman's condescending attitude and played the wrong cards. Gerald never let her forget it. After the couple left, he threw the cards in the fireplace, where they didn't burn very well at all. This made Gerald even madder. They never played cards with anyone after that.

*\*\**

Marci watches Jamie when she delivers. Her slide out of the hack is effortless, her arm straight as the horizon, her concentration fierce. Although the rules say that you have to release the rock before the hog line, this doesn't stop Jamie from sliding nearly halfway up the sheet of ice. Marci thinks she would like to look like that some day. Just for one moment, a graceful stretch of body, eyes locked on the skip's broom, the arm out in front holding a perfect line, and the release, smooth and gentle. Beautiful.

Jamie was right about the jeans, too. There's no give at all when Marci squats in the hack. This time she tries to remember Jamie's delivery, her technique, and she is shocked when one of her rocks ends up in the house. "Great shot, Marci," says Lew. "Good shootin' girl," says Jamie.

*Girl*, thinks Marci. She hasn't been called a girl like that in a long time. Gerald's disparaging names for her float on the edges of her consciousness. *Small Town Girl! Country Girl!*

But here, now, in this crystalline moment, she is once again *a girl!*

Success is fleeting. The next two ends are disappointing. She finally gets another one in the house, just a biter. Her other shots end up being casualties. It's probably a good thing they're not curling for the car.

When Scotty throws his rocks, his yelling at the far end of the ice is almost orgasmic. "Sweep, girls. Haaaard. Come on, girls, sweep your butts off. It's gotta be here." There was a time when something so politically incorrect would have set a fire under her. But not any more. She laughs along with everyone else and then goes to work with Jamie on the rock, pushing down on their brooms. It seems if you can get a certain momentum going, the sweepers can carry the rock from one end of the ice to the other. This time they succeed in bringing it in for shot, nicely tucked in behind a guard. In spite of Scotty's amazing shot making, which has rescued them from some terrible looking ends, he doesn't take himself too seriously.

"God, that was a circus shot, eh?" he says, scratching his sparse, greying hair. "Good sweeping, girls."

"Yeah, that was great," echoes Lew. He taps her shoulder with his broom in a brotherly fashion.

Marci smiles. She could grow to like these people.

The eighth end. Marci has only two more chances to redeem herself. She settles into the hack. She has to admit it's starting to feel a bit more natural, like swimming with the current instead of against it. Scotty's team is down one coming home without last rock. Suddenly, Scotty disappears. No one seems to mind. Marci guesses he's slipped out the side door to take a little nip. She wishes he'd hurry back, though. She's getting a little stiff from squatting on the ice so long. Finally, he returns. Holds his broom at the top of the twelve foot.

Marci gives herself a mental talking to. Now, keep your eye on the broom, hold your arm straight, let the rock go gently. She sends it off. Wills it to do her bidding. Finally, after much sweeping by Lew and Jamie, it nestles into the top of the twelve foot like it has arrived home. For her next rock, Scotty calls for a nice little raise. A finesse shot. She's flattered that Scotty would even think she could make such a shot. Now, concentrate, she tells herself. Don't mess up. She has visions of throwing too hard and taking her own rock out, like before. She sends it off down the ice as gently and carefully as a young mother sending her first born off to kindergarten. She taps her own back to the button for shot. Perfect. Finally, it has taken the whole game to make both her shots. Marci doesn't really care who wins the game now. She hasn't felt so alive for months. She is aware of her own body, its frailty, its clumsiness, but also its power, its return to the game.

"Do me a favour, Jamie, will you?" says Marci. "Phone me tomorrow and see if I'm still alive."

Jamie laughs. "Don't worry. You'll know you're alive when you get out of bed in the morning. Every muscle will be telling you."

"Yeah, that's what I'm afraid of."

The game over, they follow each other into the waiting room to remove their curling gear and put their winter boots and jackets on before confronting the bitter cold.

"Hey, Marci. Want to go for a beer?" Lew's leaning on his broom with both elbows. A half-smile plays across his mouth.

"Sure. Why not."

They head out into the starry night. The hotel bar is only a block away, its red neon light looking a little sad compared to the spectacular light show playing out in the night sky.

Marci pulls up her hood, balances her broom on one shoulder, and slings her gym bag over the other. She lifts her face to the heavens. On a night like this, she tries to invent her own constellations. It takes a lot of concentration, but finally it starts to come. Yes, she's got it now. She can make out the star-to-star outline of a strange night bird, all grace and line. A curler in full delivery position.

Beautiful, she thinks. Beautiful.

## Pilgrimage in Winter

Marie coaxes her eighty-two-year-old legs along the snow-caked sidewalk. It's the second week of January and winter has struck in all its meanness: -30 coupled with a killing wind chill. How she wishes she'd put her warm woolen slacks on, but no, she'd had to wear a long skirt to mass at St. Cecelia's. The old habits hang on, like burrs, refusing to let go. She can't believe what her grandchildren wear to church. If they show up at all, they're dressed to please themselves: baggy blue jeans with holes at the knees and sweatshirts with vulgar things written on them. Marie doesn't know why Father Coté even gives them communion. And on top of that, the children's mother, Regine. Yes, it's really her fault. She works as a secretary at that fancy law office downtown. Marie doesn't see how Regine can possibly have time for her children when she's so busy getting herself all spruced up for work. No wonder they leave for school in the morning looking like refugees.

One more block to go and still the cold slices into her legs where the short boots do not come up far enough, nor the tweed coat down low enough. The street is bereft of traffic and people. No one is crazy enough to be out in this unless they really have to. Marie hopes Father Coté has unlocked the church. She shuffles along, the cold a kind of hell she must escape. Whoever decided that hell is a place of unbearable heat couldn't ever have been to Saskatchewan in the dead of winter. She puts her head down, pulling her old knitted scarf around her face. If she can make it one more block, past the schoolyard, the cenotaph, and then at last: the spire of St. Cecelia's stabs the pale winter sky.

Inside the barely warm church, Marie collapses on the cushioned kneeler. Her glasses have defrosted enough so that she can just make out the other two women seated a few pews ahead of her, Mesdames Trembler and Arsenault. Together, they form The Three Holy Women of St. Cecelia's. Marie smiles to herself. She wouldn't be surprised if there's a rock group called that. Her niece has a CD by a group called Our Lady Peace, of all things. They make crazy sounding music, all noise and chaos. It seems to her as if the world has gone mad, everything turned upside down.

The church is empty except for the three of them. But it's a weekday mass, and with a shrinking congregation, not many more can be expected. The other two women always walk together, never asking Marie to join them. Bah, Marie thinks. I don't need anyone.

At last, Father Coté sweeps around from the back of the sacristy, his white alb and green chasuble fluttering behind him. Father Coté is always in a hurry. Marie notices a small white smear in the corner of his mouth. Could it be toothpaste? she wonders. He leads them through the penitential rite so quickly that Marie can barely find time to put a name to her sins. She tries to focus on the readings, the same readings she has been hearing since her days at the convent. She looks up at one of the tall, arch-shaped windows, as tall as a door, the pale winter light trying to break through, and it brings to mind another place and time, a similar window. A time when more than a hundred teenaged girls, dressed identically in shapeless black uniforms with white collars and cuffs, went to mass in the cold chapel at St. Joseph's, their meager voices raised in prayer and song. There was never any doubt in that other time that prayers were answered, that faith was constant. They were stacking up points trying to get into heaven, weren't they?

Marie especially loved the month of May, filled as it was with devotions to Mary. The old hymns still float on the edges of memory:

> Immaculate Mary your praises we sing,
> You reign now in splendour with Jesus your King.
> Ave, Ave, Ave, Maria.
> Ave, Ave, Ave, Maria.

The little grotto in the chapel that held the statue of the Blessed Virgin was always decorated with spring flowers: lilacs and peonies and irises, their scent overpowering Marie's pious thoughts, making it impossible to pray. She can almost smell them now, the flowers paying tribute to an ideal that would be impossible to live up to.

But Marie is an endless season away from spring now. "Take this all of you and drink from it: this is the cup of my blood which will be given up for you," she mumbles. To her horror she realizes she has just spoken the prayers of the consecration, sacred words that only the priest is allowed to say. Madames Trembler and Arsenault turn around and stare at her. Father Coté raises his eyebrows, as if at a naughty child.

Marie has said enough rosaries and prayed enough novenas to give her the status of sainthood, but sometimes she gets little twinges of doubt. Is anyone really listening up there?

she wonders. Do the old formulas still work? She can't believe she has lived so long and still has no answers.

She feels herself being carried inexorably into the heart of the mass: even though she has doubts sometimes, the ancient rituals have seeped into her bones. Father Coté intones in his rich baritone: "Remember, Lord, those who have gone before us marked with the sign of faith, especially those for whom we now pray." Marie makes a mental list of loved ones she has lost: sisters and brothers, a child four-years-old in a farming accident, her husband, Henri. That was twenty years ago, now. She can scarcely remember what he looked like, but she will never forget the smell of him when he came in from the fields, the smell of earth and wind.

Madame Trembler taps her on the shoulder and motions to the front. Oh dear, Marie thinks. Caught daydreaming again. Father Coté stands with the chalice holding up a host, waiting for her to come and receive it. She shuffles up to the front and holds her hands, one cupped beneath the other. Father Coté sets the sacred bread gently into her hands. "The body of Christ," he says flatly. She picks up the delicate wafer with thumb and forefinger and places it in her mouth. It is so dry and tasteless she chokes a little and then puts her head down. Ashamed. Why is she always distracted? She can't believe how hard it is to pray. What energy it takes.

After communion, the mass moves swiftly to a close. Madame Trembler with her ancient fur hat stands over her. "Come on, Marie. Time to go. Father Coté wants to lock the church."

Marie pushes her hand away.

"Very well. As you wish." Marie hears the old lady's knees crack as she genuflects and heads for the back of the church, Madame Arsenault following behind. A small procession.

Outside, Marie looks up at the spare winter sun. Can that really be the sun, or is it the moon? While she's been at mass some flat grey clouds have invaded the sky, smudging out the noontime light. She sets out. Back she goes, past the cenotaph and the schoolyard. It's still an hour before lunchtime and Jesse and Amanda won't be out of school yet. Marie wonders why those two go home for lunch anyway. All they do is fill their faces with junk food. Their mother Regine should be home giving them a good hot meal. Oh, she shouldn't be so hard on Regine. It's not all her fault. When Louis lost the farm a few years back, she had to go to work. And Louis, he found a job on an oil rig. What else were big strong farm boys good for? Marie forgets that Louis is not a boy anymore. Didn't they celebrate his forty-ninth birthday when he was home at Christmas? Can Louis really be that old? She finds it hard to believe and harder still to accept how their lives have panned out. Both Louis and Regine out chasing jobs to keep the wolves away from the door, leaving the children orphaned. There was no reason for this to happen, she thinks. Henri had left a prosperous farm. They should have been comfortable, but Louis had to have it all, all the toys. Sunk the farm in so much debt, they had lost most of it. What had made him think he had the right? she wonders. But Marie is beyond blaming now. What would be the good? She sighs and gives her attention to the street and its treasonous smoothness, its unpredictable humps and valleys.

The cold is relentless. And to make matters worse, the wind has sprung up from somewhere. Like the devil or the

88

devil's brother, lifting snow from rooftops and yards and flinging it in her face like steel edged confetti. About ten yards ahead she sees two dark shadows. Now, who would let their children out in this kind of weather? But no, as she comes closer, she sees they are two small dogs, dragging their leashes behind them. She looks around for their master, but before Marie knows what's happened, her feet are tangled in the cords and she lies sprawled on the snowy street. "Argh . . . " she cries to the dogs who take off, running happily.

The force of the fall has knocked her glasses off. Twisting her head around, Marie can see them sitting on top of a snow bank within an arm's length. She stretches out her mittened hand and clutches blindly, at last grabbing hold. Sets them on her face. Maybe it will help her get up if she can see what she's doing. She tries in vain to get purchase on the icy sidewalk, but it is so slippery she flails about. Marie's head falls back to the sidewalk with a dull thud. How long does it take before the body starts to turn to stone? Already her legs feel like lumps of wood. If anyone drives by, will they even see her, the snow is piled so high on either side of the sidewalk. Like a barricade.

She tries again to get up, but her right arm has a funny loose feeling as if it's become unhinged. The wind has already cast a gentle drift of snow over her legs. Maybe this is good. She remembers the plant man on TV saying that snow is a good insulator.

Surely someone going by will spot her soon. Jesse and Amanda will be heading home for lunch. She thinks she hears the voices of small children on the next street. She can't make out what they're saying, but she knows they are children's voices from their clarity, their brightness. Then, just as suddenly, the cries fade away.

With her ear pressed against the cold sidewalk she thinks she hears the promising sound of frozen tires connecting with snow. At last. Someone has to see her now. She tries to lift her head or at least her arm, but it is fruitless. She cannot believe it when the car passes on, thick puffs of exhaust streaming out the back end.

Marie no longer tries to get up. She looks skyward as if expecting an answer. But there are only the grey-white clouds of winter, coldly indifferent.

What is left for her to do? She curls up her small body like a fortune cookie, wrapping her old tweed coat around her legs. She stops shivering. Is this how the end comes? This silence, this letting go? She feels in her pocket for her rosary. The blue crystal one with the mother-of-pearl crucifix. She soon realizes it's not there. Must be in the other pocket, the one she's lying on with her twisted body. She knows it will be futile to try and ferret it out. What else could she use? She fingers the ten wooden buttons on her tweed coat and decides, yes, they will do. She begins to cant the devotion, the chant-like repetitions as natural as the beating of her own heart. The old ritual soothes her, and soon her mind begins to drift as if carried along by a current of water. Drifting . . . drifting across the great ocean her ancestors crossed. She had always wanted to take a pilgrimage. She'd heard about one in Ireland. What is it called? Finally the name comes to her. Lough Derg. Yes . . . that's it. A tiny island where hundreds of Catholics go every year to test their faith. Madame Trembler had tried it one year, but hadn't been strong enough to see it through. "You couldn't do it," she told Marie. "It is very hard." Pilgrims had to remove their shoes and walk on jagged rocks observing the Stations of the Cross. It was deathly cold. Then they were locked in a basilica for twenty-four hours, where they said the rosary continuously. Marie knows she would have survived.

\*\*\*

Gradually, the wind stops. It begins to snow. The flakes so soft and light, they appear unwilling to touch the ground. Marie tries to focus on just one flake, her eyes following its slow journey to the earth but she is too tired, all of her meager strength flowing into her freezing fingers as they clutch the wooden buttons. *Hail Mary full of grace, the Lord is with thee.*

## Finding Her Balance

The summer Clarisse and Barry decided to go back to Ministikiwin, Clarisse wondered if this was a dangerous thing to do: returning to a perfect place, expecting it to be the same. She remembered a gem of a lake with sandy beaches, camp spots screened by birch and pine and poplar, and the loons calling across the blue-green waters.

But Barry had insisted. They'd have fun, he said. He wanted to go water-skiing again. He hadn't water-skied since the last time they'd been at Ministikiwin, twelve years ago with the kids. Their last family holiday together. He had talked their son, Mark, and his wife, Nicole, into coming as well. Their other children, Daryl and Louise, were off creating their own adventures, Louise teaching English in Japan, and Daryl on a canoe trip in northern Saskatchewan.

Mark and Nicole had gone ahead in the motor home and Clarisse and Barry had followed behind in the car. The days before they left had been frantic, cleaning the motor home, packing it and overhauling the boat. Clarisse had spent one entire afternoon helping Barry install new steering cables. It had been a wickedly hot day and poor Barry practically had to stand on his head to get the job done.

Clarisse leaned back against the soft upholstery and sighed. She looked out at the harmless clouds scudding across a watercolour blue sky, at the hopeful green fields of wheat and barley and at the pastures of grass and alfalfa where horses lazily grazed. Clarisse liked to believe the horses were there just so passers-by like themselves could have something to admire. She felt contentment rise and fill her soul to the very margins.

Barry bent towards her and squeezed her arm. "How are you feeling, Hon? Going to try water-skiing?"

She smiled. Ever since her illness in the spring, Barry had been more than compassionate. At times he couldn't do enough for her. She only hoped it would last. Not that Barry was a cad or anything, it's just that, until her illness, their relationship had become like any other middle-aged couple's. A bit jaded. All that had changed since her diagnosis this spring. No one in the family ever say the word, as if by not giving it a name, it somehow doesn't exist. But it's always there, clinging and devious.

She had decided to put on a brave face. For Barry. And the kids.

"Oh, I don't know. I'm getting a little old for that, don't you think?" she said.

"Hey, I'm a few years older than you."

"Yes, but you're a good skier," said Clarisse. "It was never really my thing. I always used to try it once around the lake just to make you happy."

"And here all these years I thought you were having fun," said Barry.

"I was always a little scared. I really didn't want to know what it would feel like to wipe out and hit the water at fifty miles per hour."

"That's okay, Hon. You don't have to go if you don't want to."

"We'll see," Clarisse said.

The past few months had been hard on everyone, Barry's sudden disappearances out to the garage or down to the basement. When he returned, she could tell by his red swollen eyes, he'd been crying. The first night they had found out about the diagnosis, Barry had held her so tightly she thought she would break, and that night they had made love with a fierceness and a kind of desperation. As if there would be no more summers.

You always think it will never happen to you. Cancer. Clarisse had even looked the word up in the dictionary one day after the diagnosis. *A zodiacal constellation between Gemini and Leo usually pictured as a crab; a malignant tumour that tends to spread in the body, a malignant evil that spreads destructively.* It was this last definition that intrigued Clarisse. How did you fight against evil? To the best of her knowledge, she had always done everything right. Exercised daily, didn't drink or smoke, ate healthy, mostly fat-free meals. And her reward was a belligerent carcinoma, roughly the size and shape of a small plum.

Just ahead up the highway was St. Walburg, a pretty little northern town with well-kept homes and thriving gardens. Barry pulled into the Esso station for gas. He got out to wash the windows while the attendant filled the car. Clarisse stepped out for some fresh air. Already, she could smell something different. What was it? A mixture of alfalfa, pine trees, and a strange metallic odour.

She watched Barry make small talk with the gas attendant, a gangly teenager in clothes that were too big for him. How like Barry to insist on washing his own windows. At fifty-five Barry was still in pretty good shape, although lately, Clarisse had noticed how the flesh on his neck hung loosely, probably because he had lost weight. Clarisse attributed it to stress. On the farm, they seemed to lurch from one crisis to the next and then on top of it all, her illness. Clarisse went into the gas station and bought some red twizzlers for Barry and some chocolate-coated peanuts for herself. Chocolate was always a consolation and the peanuts, well; they were full of protein, weren't they?

They continued on their way. As they went farther north, the trees began filling up the landscape, edging out the cultivated fields. The sky seemed smaller and more closed in. By early afternoon, they drove through the town and past the Indian reserve, over the hill, and down to the lake. The view coming over the rise never failed to take Clarisse's breath away: the sun glinting off the water, the little islands covered in pines marooned out in the bay. They took the road past the double row of cabins that led out to the Stabler Point Campground.

At the registration booth, the impossibly young park attendant leaned out the window and told Clarisse and Barry that they'd lucked out because she'd given Mark and Nicole one of the best campsites in the whole place. Number seventy-five. Right on the lake front, maybe two hundred yards from the beach. Clarisse wasn't sure, but she thought maybe they'd stayed there once before. They looped back and forth along the trails looking for the assigned site. Clarisse noticed the birch and poplars had thinned out a little. Had there been some kind of disease, or had the armyworms been at it again? Through the trees the water flashed momentarily. Clarisse rolled her window down and took a deep breath. It was one of the things she liked most about this place. The smell. How to describe it? A blend of pine trees, lake water, the remains of campfires, and decaying undergrowth.

Just ahead, a kid maybe ten or twelve careened around the corner on a bike. Barry had to veer the car sharply to avoid hitting him.

"God, those kids," said Barry.

"Now, don't you remember when our two boys used to do the same thing?" said Clarisse. "Did you notice the bike jump when we came in? It's still there, right by the boat launch."

"We sure used to have fun here, didn't we?" said Barry. He gave her shoulder a small hug. Clarisse leaned into him for a minute.

"There's the motorhome up ahead," she said.

Nicole and Mark had already parked the RV on the level and were busy laying out the tent.

"I can't believe we got this lucky, Mom," said Mark. "What a great spot, eh?" Her lean-limbed son had taken charge of the campsite already: he had a substantial supply of wood stacked by the metal fireplace and their coolers piled neatly on the picnic table. Her son, the perfectionist. When things didn't turn out as planned, he usually beat himself up pretty badly.

Clarisse smiled. It broke her heart to see Mark trying so hard to have a good time. If anyone deserved a vacation, it was him. This past summer, working sixteen-hour days for weeks on end had drained him. She could not escape the fact that the farm was consuming them all. She prayed Mark would wake up some morning and head off in a new direction, but she wasn't holding her breath.

Clarisse helped Nicole count out the tent pegs, making sure they were all there. Nicole, with her bobbed, sun-streaked blond hair topped by a faded ball cap, her slim tanned legs sprouting out of blue-jean cut-offs, was being a good sport about the camp trip. She'd probably've preferred a holiday with friends her own age, Clarisse mused. She looked at her with a strange mixture of envy and admiration.

"Remember, Mom, that summer Daryl got lost?" Mark asked. "How old was he anyway?" He fiddled with the metal poles for the tent, trying to figure out how they went together. Barry was giving him a hand.

"I don't remember," said Clarisse. "Maybe eight or nine."

"Daryl was always taking off in those days," Mark said. "I wonder what he was looking for."

Clarisse thought about that summer Daryl had got lost. How they'd panicked because there had been several bear sightings in the area. How they'd been lucky enough to enlist the help of one of Barry's cousins who lived nearby, and who just happened to be visiting the campsite and was an excellent tracker and woodsman. He had taken off on foot and before too long was back with a sheepish Daryl in tow. Daryl. Always off searching for something while Mark seemed tethered to home.

Mark and Barry had the poles fitted into the right spots now and were raising the tent. Barry was covered in perspiration. "Christ, this is too hard for an old man to do anymore."

"Oh, Dad," said Mark. "Get out of the whine cellar."

Clarisse sat at the picnic table and watched her men bantering. She looked down to the lake. They had their own footpath winding through the birch and poplar, the wild roses and choke cherry bushes. It led to a small inlet where they could tie up their boat. There was even a weathered bench perched at the water's edge, the red paint peeling away. After they'd raised the tent, Mark and Barry and Nicole went to launch the boat. Clarisse picked her way down to the lake. She eased herself onto the bench, checking for slivers, stretched out her bare arms and legs to the sun, embracing its heat. She ran her fingers through her short chaotic hair. Pulled on her bangs to straighten them out. As usual, they had a funny little kink. She thought her legs looked anemic but mused about the wisdom of sunbathing. Out on the lake, a red canoe headed towards the narrows. Clarisse watched until her eyes grew dazed by the sun. She wondered if this would be the last time they would come to the lake together. She pushed her sunglasses back up on her nose with the back of her hand and was not surprised to find her face wet with tears.

Shading her eyes against the mid-afternoon sun, Clarisse could make out their little sixteen-foot outboard cutting across the water. It had been a good boat, had pulled all the kids around the lake on skis for many summers. Clarisse liked the way it hugged the water, refusing to rear up like some of the bigger, more powerful boats. Something seemed to be wrong with the steering, though. At times, it was as if Barry wasn't sure what direction to go. Clarisse stood up on the shore and waved. Finally, Barry cut the motor, and used the oars to bring the boat back to shore. He threw her the yellow nylon rope. She grabbed hold and hand-over-hand began pulling him in. Barry jumped out to give her a hand.

"Shit," said Barry. "I put the goddamn steering cables in backwards."

"Oh, Barry. How did that happen?"

"Damned if I know."

By this time Nicole and Mark had returned from the launch with the motor home and were heading down the footpath to join them.

Barry was already under the bow of the boat, disconnecting the cables. "What's wrong now?" asked Mark.

"The cables somehow got put in backwards," said Clarisse.

"Geez." Mark rolled his eyes. "Can't he do anything right any more?"

"Take it easy, Mark," Clarisse said quietly. "He's had a lot on his mind lately."

"Yeah," said Nicole. "Let it go." The two women looked at each other. Nicole smiled. "Come on, Clarisse," she said. "Let's go check out the beach."

They walked single-file, following the trail that cut through the forest down to the lake. Clarisse noticed small changes. The huge rock, which used to sit at the water's edge where the three kids posed every year for a picture, had been removed. The floating raft, which had been anchored out in the swimming area, had disappeared. Clarisse recalled how she and the other women would swim out to the raft and sun themselves for hours, pretending they were marooned on a romantic island. She also noticed a strange, white scum where the water engaged the shore. Twelve years ago, the lake had been clear as Perrier.

The two women plopped down on a shabby wooden bench. Clarisse took off her Birkenstocks, covered her toes with sand. Colourful umbrellas were scattered like wildflowers across the stretch of beach. Sunbathers were much more responsible these days, it seemed. Clarisse watched a young mother just in front of them stake a claim to several square meters of beach. She had pushed a rather large stroller that doubled as a U-Haul. Clarisse couldn't believe the provisions the young mother extracted from it. Blankets, bags of food and drink, plastic beach toys, and of course, an umbrella. She assumed there must be a baby in the stroller somewhere. The young mother took charge immediately, spreading out a huge blanket made from scraps of old blue jeans. How clever, thought Clarisse. The woman dug a hole with her son's plastic shovel and inserted the pole of the umbrella. The hole was a bit too shallow and a gust of wind caught the umbrella, making it fly up and hit Clarisse in the chest. She winced and threw her arms up, her hands automatically going to the place where her breast used to be.

"Oh, I'm so sorry," said the woman. She rushed to where Nicole and Clarisse were sitting and rescued the umbrella from taking off again.

"No problem," said Clarisse. She handed the flying missile back to the woman.

"You okay, Clarisse?" said Nicole. She rested a hand gently on her knee.

"Fine. I'm fine." Clarisse took a deep breath.

Nicole touched her arm. "Look," she said. "There's our boat. I wonder if they figured out the steering cables yet."

Clarisse shook her head. "That boat was always a tinker's delight. Come on, Nicole. Let's go and see if they're ready to ski."

They picked their way back to the little cove where Mark and Barry were busy attaching the ski-rope to the back of the boat.

"Wanta go first?" asked Barry, smiling at Clarisse.

"Are you kidding?" she said. " I don't know if I'm going to go at all." She waded into the water, splashing it up on her legs to see how cold it was.

"You're not? Come on, Hon. Be a sport. It'll be good for you." He continued untangling the rope, feeding it out to the back of the boat.

"Mom, are you going first?" asked Mark. "Show us how it's done?"

"Yeah, right," said Clarisse. "Tomorrow. Maybe." Just thinking about getting up on skis was sending little shivers up the backs of her legs.

Nicole had gone up to the campsite to get the skis, while Mark filled the tank with gas.

"Why don't you be the spotter, Hon?" asked Barry.

"Sure thing," said Clarisse. She figured this was one way to get out of skiing. She shrugged herself into a life jacket. Her chest still hurt from the surgery last winter. And from the flying umbrella.

Mark dunked himself in the cold lake water and then leaned back to put his skis on. He was signaling them to take off. "Go," he shouted. "Go."

The boat fought the weight of the water, trying to pull Mark up. Clarisse looked back and smiled. Fifteen years ago, all the kids had come up easily, like little corks. But Mark probably weighed twice as much today. Little wonder the boat was having trouble. Finally, he surfaced. Lurched backwards momentarily, and then they were off. Barry pulled his ball cap down to shade his eyes from the water's glare. He refused to bother with sunglasses, thinking they were accessories that only movie stars wore.

They cruised once around the small lake and then Barry headed off around the peninsula over to Jumbo Beach. There weren't many water skiers out today. Mostly seadoers that buzzed around in front of them, making waves.

"Damn it," said Barry. "Why don't they go somewhere else?"

Clarisse wondered about Mark's hockey-damaged knees, if they would be able to withstand the stress of water-skiing, but he looked strong and confident as he skimmed over the waves. Clarisse gave him the thumbs-up sign and got a big grin in return. She'd forgotten how much fun it was to watch her kids play, remembering when Mark had been centre for the Dynamos, his wide set eyes allowing him to scope in on the puck, setting up his teammates for goal after goal. He hadn't played hockey for years now.

After Mark signalled to go in, Barry circled the little island and pointed the boat towards the cove where Clarisse could see Nicole sitting on the bench. Two red buoys marked the spot where they could tie up the boat. Mark let go of the rope and glided the last fifty meters, nearly skiing up to the shoreline. Nicole applauded. Mark pulled off the skis and let out a victory yell. "Too bad old Daryl isn't here to see me now, eh Mom? Okay, Dad. Your turn."

He switched places with his father. Clarisse didn't know if this was such a great idea. Barry hadn't skied since they'd come to the lake twelve years ago. But he was game; it didn't take him long to pull the skis on. He was just about ready to go, when Mark yelled, "Hey, Dad. You forgot to take your hat off."

Nicole swam out to retrieve it, jammed it on her head and swam back in again. How like him, thought Clarisse, to leave on that damn hat. Even when he got dressed up for a funeral or a wedding, he insisted on wearing his ball cap until they reached the church.

She was surprised at how easily Barry came up out of the water. At first he stayed behind the wake where it was calm, but before long, he was veering off to the side where it was faster. Once when Mark turned the boat a little too quickly and caught his dad off-guard, he teetered for a second, and then regained his balance. Clarisse smiled. Barry's wild new trunks, a collage of psychedelic green and orange and pink, were made to camouflage a full-figured man and were somewhat loose on him. They looked like small sails attached to his torso, whipping in the wind. A spin around the small lake and then once around the big lake and Barry gave the signal to go in.

Then it was Nicole's turn. Clarisse envied the way she so effortlessly cut back and forth across the waves. If only she could do the same. She thought how easy it would be to have confidence if you looked like that. Clarisse glanced down at her own body, her pale thin legs, her flabby arms, her protruding stomach. She felt betrayed.

Mark was taking up the cause again. "Come on, Mom. You're the only one who hasn't gone now. It's your turn."

"Maybe tomorrow," she replied. "It's been a pretty full day already."

Nicole glided to a stop, full of strength and grace.

Mark looped back to the shore, then cut the motor. Clarisse pulled the yellow towrope in, hand over hand. Grabbing one of the paddles, she helped Mark row them in. Mark jumped out and pulled the boat safely up on the beach and then fastened the rope securely around a sturdy birch tree.

All three of them were so proud of themselves, they swaggered up to the campsite wearing silly grins. Clarisse couldn't help smiling herself.

"Are you sure you don't want to try it today?" Barry asked.

"Tomorrow, eh Mom?" teased Mark. How anxious they all were for her to succeed.

Clarisse looked down at the lake. Most of the boats had given up for the day. Suddenly, it was quiet. Tomorrow, she'd try. Maybe tomorrow.

***

The next day was cloudy and cool. In spite of this, Clarisse and Nicole insisted on setting up camp on the beach. They brought their blankets and books and a cooler of drinks and snacks. They tried to convince themselves they were having a good time. And once in a great while, the sun would break through the clouds and reward them for their patience with two minutes of sunshine. The cool day hadn't stopped Barry and Mark from water-skiing. They were off somewhere together.

Clarisse supposed she better give it a try today. Just so they'd leave her alone. She was running out of tomorrows. She laid her open book across her midriff and looked across to where the lake turned to follow the south shoreline. Several children were playing in the shallow water there, in an aimless, haphazard way. The way children sometimes do. The water had taken on a strange, dark green cast, almost black. It gave her the shivers. At the edges of her consciousness she felt a small jab of fear. She tried to nudge it away. Realized with clarity it wasn't herself she was afraid for, it was her family. How would they manage without her? When the time came. Who would be there to give Mark a little extra push to bolster his confidence? Who would rein Daryl in when he wandered too far into the stratosphere? Who would hold Barry in the middle of the night?

The children, silhouettes now more than clear figures, continued to run in and out of the water. She could hear their cries drift across the lake. Ragged bits of sound lost in the din from the motorboats.

\*\*\*

Mark and Barry were back with the boat. Barry had the motor cover off and was tinkering with what looked to be spark plugs. Clarisee couldn't be sure at this distance.

Mark yelled across, "Mom, you gonna try today? Better get in the water and get used to it. It's a bit cold."

Nicole pulled her up off the beach blanket. "Come on, Clarisse. No more excuses. Let's get wet and then you can try it." She raced into the lake and dove under in one easy movement. "It's great. Come in," she yelled.

Clarisse waded in up to her knees, gauging the temperature. Cold. Oh, what the hell, she thought. I might as well go for it. She plunged in and under, the water closing over her head, roaring in her ears. She surfaced and swam out into the lake several meters until she'd caught up to Nicole.

"It's not that bad, is it?" Nicole said.

"No," answered Clarisse, treading water."But, you have to keep moving." She had lost a lot of weight and with it her insulation.

"I'm going to swim over to the boat and see if they're ready to ski," said Nicole. She swam off executing a perfect forward crawl. Clarisse loved the way she moved. She wished they'd hurry up and fix the boat. She didn't know how much longer she would last in this temperature. She was starting to shake already.

"Okay," yelled Barry. "I think we're ready." He was in his element when fixing something. The only thing he couldn't fix was her.

Clarisse swam over and grabbed a life jacket. Her fingers were so cold she had trouble tying the cord. She hoped it would keep her afloat. Nicole was appointed spotter while Mark helped Clarisse into the awkward skis. Then she shuffled out until the water was up to her armpits, leaned back and grabbed the towrope. Tried to bring her skis up and hold them straight. They felt so heavy.

"It's okay, Mom. I'm here," said Mark. He held the skis vertically and then gave Barry the signal to go.

Clarisse urged her body up and out of the water. Realized she had pulled too hard and suddenly she was headfirst in the lake. This was not going to be easy.

She scrambled to collect her skis and fought to put them on again. Barry circled around so the towrope brushed against her. She lunged for it, grabbed on and fought with the skis again. Then gave him the signal to go. She remembered Barry telling her it was all about balance. This time she got up and then fell backwards into the lake.

She was cold. Her body trembling.

They were farther from shore now. Each time she'd fallen had dragged them out into more dangerous water. Unpredictable seadoos. Crazy kids on rubber tubes being pulled by too-fast boats.

Barry yelled across, "Maybe you better go in, Hon. Don't overdo it." He was idling the boat, trying to keep it from drifting away from her.

Suddenly, she felt a well of anger rise to the surface. Anger at herself for being so powerless. At them for their well-intentioned kindness that threatened to paralyze her.

"One more time, damn it," she shouted.

She could barely find the strength to push her feet into the stiff rubber boots of the skis, but at last she had them on again. Her leg muscles screamed in agony and her arms felt as if they were being pulled out of their sockets, but she managed to bring her skis up pointing at the sky. Grabbed the towrope and flipped it up between her legs, prepared for take-off. "Ready," she shouted. "Go."

***

They sat around the campfire later than usual that night, each one reluctant to break the spell. They were all tired; most of all, Clarisse. She didn't look forward to tomorrow morning, to the aching muscles. It would be brutal. She knew this was the last time she would water-ski. But she was glad she had persevered. If only she could make an imprint of that feeling she'd had riding the waves. It wasn't about control at all. It was about letting go. That was the key.

She shifted in her lawn chair. Yawned. Time to turn in.

"Come on, Hon," said Barry. "Bedtime. We better let these young people alone for a spell."

"Oh, Dad," protested Mark.

"Maybe we better make a trip to the washroom before turning in, eh?" said Barry.

"Good idea," said Clarisse.

Together they started up the trail. Most of the campsites had shut down for the night, but there was the odd family still circled around a glowing fire. Clarisse could barely see the lake through the trees, the dark pines blacking out the silent, silvery water. But she could hear two loons calling across the lake, their ancient, lonely cry penetrating her soul.

They stopped on the footpath, looking down to the lake, listening to the loons. Barry wrapped both arms around her in a bear hug. "You're safe and sound with me,'" he said. Clarisse leaned into his shoulder. Smelled the wood smoke in his quilted flannel shirt. She stroked his face, rough with a day's growth of whiskers.

Then, they turned from the lake and walked on into the night.

# Julie

## 1. Haying Season

It was Friday night and so they found themselves in the bar at the Rainbow Ridge Hotel. Julie, Tanya and Michelle pulled their chairs up to the circular table and leaned their elbows on the terrycloth table covers. They were all teachers at Glendale Composite. Single. And even though they were more than a decade apart in age, they shared stories from school about delinquent kids or impossible parents or inept administration. Sometimes they shared a rubbery pizza or greasy hamburgers cooked up by the hotelkeeper's wife.

It was June twenty-ninth, the last day of school, and they felt the same relief they'd experienced themselves on the last day of school, five or ten or twenty years ago, depending on which woman you were talking about.

Gerry McGraw, owner and bartender, bounced over to take their orders. He was a short middle-aged balding man with a dirty tan in Bermuda shorts and a golf shirt.

An aluminum tray balanced on his hip, he enquired, "What'll it be, girls?"

"Labatt's Lite," Julie said automatically.

"Double that," said Michelle.

They both turned to look at Tanya who always tried to order something the bar didn't carry. Julie wondered if it was intentional — perhaps to make the bartender feel inferior. An outsider's way to let everyone know that she was a woman of the world?

"Do you have any Corona?" Tanya played with the little gold chain around her neck.

"No. No, I don't," he said. "Sorry." He shifted his tray to his other hip while Tanya made up her mind. He looked amused.

Tanya seemed puzzled for a moment. "Oh, that's okay. Make it a Canadian."

The three women leaned into the padded chairs and sighed collectively. For two entire months, with any luck, the biggest decision they'd have to make would be what kind of beer to order. Summer was an empty calendar: no more lesson plans, or papers to grade, or kids to discipline. Discipline? The word didn't exist anymore, let alone the concept. Classroom management. That's what it was called now.

"Well," said Michelle. "I'm glad another grad has come and gone without too much incident. Except for the graffiti." She was referring to the huge Grad 2000 sign spray painted on the skylight in the school's atrium the night before.

Tanya snorted. "Yeah, it's a wonder they didn't kill themselves up there. They were probably drunk."

"No doubt," said Julie. "Whoever it was had to know enough to write backwards so we could read it though. Amazing. I don't know if I could do that."

"Maybe it was one of your special ed. English kids," said Michelle. "One who's dyslexic or something."

They all laughed.

Gerry was back with their beer and they were quiet for a minute or so. Julie wrapped her hands around the cool frosted glass; sipped greedily. She was thirsty and the beer tasted good.

Tanya got up to plug the jukebox. Oh please, thought Julie, don't play some head banging piece of shit. Please, not today. God, she must be getting old if loud music bothered her. She was surprised when Eric Clapton's "Tears in Heaven" came threading out of the jukebox. Tanya swayed back to the table, hips gyrating, mouthing the words.

"Is that too crazy for you ladies?" she asked. Heavy accent on the ladies. She straddled the chair backwards and continued to move her hips in time to the music.

"You all packed, Tanya?" asked Julie.

"Yep. She's all done. Just gotta drop my empties off at the Liquor Board. Finish packing my clothes and then I'm outa here."

Tanya was the phys. ed teacher at the school, the latest in a long string of them, most of them sticking it out for a year, before they moved up the career ladder. She'd landed a position in Saskatoon for the fall term. A six-month contract, but she was hoping it would mutate into something more permanent.

Julie'd been teaching in Glendale eighteen years this fall. She'd grown up on the farm just ten miles north of town up the valley road and had come back to her hometown to teach; it had seemed like a good idea at the time. Glendale had been a booming little place, farming was good, the town was growing. Back then it had a hospital, an implement dealer, a drugstore, two garages, a cafe. Now, everything was changed. What with subsidy wars, grain prices in the toilet, and the climbing cost of inputs, farmers were pulling out in droves, selling out or going broke. Of course they didn't encourage their kids to take up farming, either; it would have been considered child abuse. Julie's parents had sold the farm a few years back and moved to Swift Current, closer to a hospital.

Julie couldn't really have said why she ended up staying so long. Unless it was some kind of gravitational pull that she had no control over. She'd always thought it would be nice to settle down in her own home town amongst family and friends, but now it seemed as if even they were deserting her. And besides, there just weren't many job opportunities left for teachers her age. They wanted someone young, like Tanya, whom they could pay nothing and bully into organizing all the extracurricular activities.

A few stragglers wandered into the bar: a couple of farmers in jeans and ball caps and faded, misshapen T-shirts. Their faces bright red from sun and wind, they looked thirsty and tired. They'd probably been haying — it was the season for it. Julie'd had a run-in with one of them a few years back. He'd taken her to task over making his boy read so many books when he should have been home helping with the harvest. What was the kid's name anyway? Jason. That was it. Jason Barnsley from north of town. He'd quit school in grade nine, Julie remembered. She supposed he hadn't picked up a book since.

A bunch of guys from the pipeline crew had staked out a table behind the women. If Mother Nature called, the women would have to rub shoulders with them to get to the bathroom. Julie shivered and unconsciously crossed her legs; she had a good bladder. The girls huddled together ignoring both tables of men.

Julie looked around at the shabby bar as if she was seeing it for the first time: the cheap imitation wallboard which reflected the hard light, the chrome chairs with cracked vinyl seats, the red and black velvet wallpaper calling to mind a New Orleans's bordello, the rogue's gallery of local sports teams tacked up on the wall, hockey and baseball and curling heroes.

Michelle waved her hand in front of Julie's face. "Earth to Julie. Earth to Julie. Come in." Julie gave herself a little shake. She hadn't realized she was daydreaming. "What are you doing this summer?" Michelle asked.

"No plans really. Just a little R&R."

"You're coming to my wedding, aren't you?" asked Michelle. "The end of July, remember?"

"Oh yeah, sure. I'll be there." She noticed a button undone on her denim skirt, just above knee level. She quickly did it up and then glanced at the pipeliners beside them hoping they hadn't noticed.

Michelle had taught school in Glendale for ten years, a weird combination of science, math, home-ec and drama. She was getting married to an engineer who worked in a diamond mine in northern Alberta. Three weeks in. One week out. Julie didn't envy Michelle, her lonely life stuck in Edmonton by herself. She hoped Michelle hadn't panicked and grabbed onto something that wouldn't work out. Thirty was about the age that women panicked if they weren't married. Especially in a small town. And at thirty-eight, Julie's age, just about the whole town stopped hoping. People quit trying to fix her up with every newcomer that wandered in. And as time went on, Julie could see her chances being cut down as surely as the hay crops in the fields and ditches.

"So, any other craziness happen last night?" asked Julie.

"It was a safe grad party, so everything probably went all right," said Michelle. "It's the party tonight and the one tomorrow night the parents should worry about."

"Right," said Julie. "It's such a farce, isn't it?" She didn't tell the girls about coming across some cars in her early morning walk with half-asleep occupants in various states of undress. She'd walked on quickly. Embarrassed. She had no intention of finding out for sure who they were. She didn't want to know; maybe they were even some of her students. Besides, she believed sex was a sacred thing; it should be anointed with silence. It was years ago now that Julie'd had an affair with the science teacher, Grant Sonmor. Talk about chemistry. They'd tried to keep it quiet but in a small town that was just about impossible. The self-righteous parents and the over-zealous school board eventually put a stop to it. Grant left town that summer and went overseas to teach English. She never saw him again. After that, it was like a small faucet inside Julie had been turned off.

The bartender showed up with a tray of drinks and set them around the table. "Compliments of these nice fellas beside you here." He winked and motioned to the pipeline workers.

When the girls turned to look, all three guys tipped their hats in an exaggerated kind of way. They weren't huddled around the table like the women; they sprawled out, arms open wide across the backs of their chairs, legs spread apart, calling attention to themselves.

"Oh, shit," said Julie. She could see what was coming down the line. Three young guys in their twenties. Friday night. The testosterone count rising with every beer they drank. She glanced at Tanya; she'd be the one they'd be gunning for. Julie was out of the running now and Michelle was already spoken for.

"Be careful, girl," she said quietly to Tanya.

"Yes, mother." Tanya rolled her eyes and giggled.

"Here," said Julie. "Get a bag of chips or something." She threw some money on the table. "I've gotta go to the Ladies."

One of the pipeline workers, the one with the serpent tattoo on his forearm, was blocking her path to the washroom.

"Excuse me," Julie said, trying not to sound like a bitchy schoolteacher.

"Pardon me, ma'am." He jumped up from his chair and made an elaborate sweeping motion with his hairy arm while Julie passed through. She brushed against him, close enough to catch an odour of beer and sweat and machine oil.

In the bathroom she squatted on the toilet while holding her foot against the door. Ever since she started coming in this bar twenty years ago, the lock hadn't worked. Julie relaxed and put her foot down. Who was she afraid of anyway? The only other women in the bar were Michelle and Tanya. And those other cowboys out there? She didn't think they'd had that much to drink; they should still know the difference between the men and women's bathroom.

She read the graffiti: "Melanie's a hoe." "Daryl is mine. Keep your hands off him." It served as a community bulletin board of sorts. Underneath the layers of paint Julie could probably find some graffiti she'd written herself when she first started coming into the bar.

She ran lukewarm water over her hands from the corroded tap before realizing there were no paper towels. She wiped them on her denim skirt instead. Looked in the mirror above the sink. The light was ghastly. She tried to do a quick makeover by smearing a coat of lipstick on her too-thin lips — Downtown Brown it was called, from Mary Kaye. She flicked her short-cropped hair behind her ears. Shit, who was she doing this for, anyway? She leaned into the mirror and met her deep violet eyes staring back at her. She looked like someone waiting for something to happen, she thought, and then quickly pushed the thought aside.

She shouldered her way through the bathroom door, back to the bar. In the brief time span she'd been gone, the atmosphere had changed. The music had been cranked up; everyone was talking louder. Tanya had defected to the table with the pipeline workers leaving Michelle orphaned.

"Sorry, Michelle," said Julie. "Didn't mean to desert you. What's with Tanya?"

"Oh, she's just having a little fun, I guess, before leaving town tomorrow." She laughed.

"Well, I'm sure as hell not staying around to babysit her," said Julie.

"Don't worry about Tanya. She can take care of herself." Michelle yawned.

"You ready to go?" asked Julie. "Suppose you got a lot of things at home to do before you take off."

"I've got all the small stuff packed. Jeff will be up tomorrow with the U-Haul for all the bigger things." Michelle stretched. Her eyes had a faraway look, as if she was already in another country.

"Let's go, then," said Julie. They pushed back their chairs. On the way out they stopped at the pipeliners' table.

"Keep in touch, eh Tanya," said Julie. "Drop us an e-mail sometime."

Tanya stood up and the three of them had a group hug. "Have a good life," said Tanya. "I'm going miss you both so much."

Julie walked home, the smell of freshly cut hay moving in from the edge of town. She would always associate that smell with the end of things and the pain of new beginnings.

***

The next morning Julie stayed in bed an extra hour to celebrate the beginning of the holidays. It felt good to let her mind go blank after spending months crowding it with lesson plans and schedules and deadlines. Her bedroom faced east so she could tell by the light the time of day; probably about nine o'clock. She was pleased with herself for staying in bed so long.

Then she remembered it was Saturday. Sid's Garage only stayed open 'til noon. She better get down there and get the tire fixed on the Tempo before he closed. She'd happened to notice it was flat when she got home from the bar last night.

She only lived a block from Sid's. She could take the tire off, roll it down the street, get it fixed, and then roll it back again. She dressed quickly in a pair of coverall shorts and a T-shirt, pulled a comb through her hair, stopping to look in the mirror for a few seconds only. The mirror was hung too low for Julie's basketball-player height and it annoyed her that she had to stoop every time she looked in it. Tall, and slim as a stiletto. At least she had that much going for her, she thought.

Julie knew how to change a tire; her dad had made sure of that. An only daughter, and if she was going to help out on the farm, she better be able to take care of herself. Julie put the emergency brake on, then got the jack and tire iron out of the trunk. She loosened the bolts easily, and then jacked up the car to finish the job. She'd once thought of training for a mechanic. But twenty years ago girls didn't do things like that. Especially in small towns. And in a way, her independence had scared off a lot of guys.

She wiggled the dusty tire off the axle. It dropped to the ground and then sagged against her legs with a thud. A little cloud of dust puffed up settling on her sandled feet.

Rolling a flat tire up the street was a little like pushing a stone uphill. Julie doubled over and tried to build momentum. Once, it veered off into the street and she had to wrestle it back into line. She was very conscious of her six feet span of body bent awkwardly in two.

As she passed the big front window at Sid's, she could see three guys sitting on stools grouped around the counter. Coffeebreak time. Just my luck, she thought. She rolled the tire through the big overhead doors and let it bounce to its resting spot on the cracked cement floor.

"Sid," she yelled.

Sid poked his head in from the office door where he was taking his coffee break. He was the town godfather. Everyone went to Sid with their troubles; people could count on him not to spread their most intimate secrets to the next fella. Farmers who were having trouble making their payments, fathers with delinquent kids, guys who were upset with their women folk. He was a guy you could count on. This past winter, Sid had had a stroke. Not a real bad one but it had left his right arm without much mobility. He still came to work every day, though; the locals counted on him to be there. The guys were good to Sid. They let him do what he could and stepped in to give him a hand only after he asked.

"What did you bring me there, Julie?" Sid glanced at the tire in the middle of the shop. "Oh, a flat tire? Gosh, Julie, it doesn't look so bad. It's only flat on one side." He chuckled at his own joke.

Julie smiled. Sid had said the same thing the last time she came in with a flat tire.

"Let's have a look and see what we got here."

Sid located the problem; a small innocent looking nail had punctured the tire. It would have to be taken off the rim to be fixed. Julie stood by and looked on while Sid struggled with the tire.

Finally he said, "Come on Julie, you got two good arms. Come and give an old man a hand."

She was only too glad to help out. She added her muscle to his and pulled on the bar until the tire popped off.

"Atta girl," said Sid. "Hey, you looking for a job? I might need someone this summer."

Julie pushed her glasses back up on her nose; it was sweltering in the garage. She didn't know how Sid could stand wearing overalls in this heat, but she guessed they were a necessary evil. She noticed her hands were greasy already from helping him.

"Thanks for giving me a hand, Julie," said Sid. "Go and sit with the boys in the office, there. I'll have a patch on in no time."

Julie shoved her dirty hands in her pockets and leaned in the office doorway.

Three middle-aged farmers sat in companionable silence holding Styrofoam cups. They looked up at Julie and grinned.

"Nice make-up job, Julie," said Ray Fines, a lanky fellow in cowboy boots, who sat with his long legs entwined around an old metal stool.

"Make-up job?" She couldn't remember putting on any make-up this morning. She went and looked in the side mirror of an old half-ton sitting in the garage waiting to be fixed. She laughed when she saw the black streak of grease running down her nose.

Sid was laughing, too. "Here, Julie." He handed her a paper towel with some degreaser on it. "Your tire's all done." He motioned to the three coffee drinkers." Why don't one of you guys here give Julie a hand to put it back on?"

Ray Fines unwound his skinny legs from the bar stool and stood looking down on Julie. There weren't too many men who could do that.

"Sure," said Ray. "I'll just put it in the back of the half-ton and drop it off at your place. I can help you put it back on too, if you like."

Julie blushed. "Oh, no, that won't be necessary. I can manage. But I'd be grateful if you'd drop it off. The little white stucco at the end of this block going west." She felt stupid after she'd told him where she lived. Of course, he'd already know that. She must be nervous.

"Sure thing," said Ray. He lifted his ball cap, finger-combed his thick red hair, and then repositioned the hat on his head. He seemed to find her independence amusing.

"Julie here's going to come and crank wrenches for me this summer," said Sid. "She's quite the girl." He winked at the men.

"Thanks Sid," said Julie. "Just put the repair bill on my tab."

She jumped in the cab of Ray's truck. She felt self-conscious; it had been so long since she'd been alone with a man she was tongue-tied.

She tried to think of something to say on the short ride to her place. Ray Fines. What did she know about him? He'd been married once, briefly, to a little twig of a girl who wore spandex shorts and skimpy tops. She'd left him shortly after they'd had their first kid. A city girl who just couldn't adjust to the isolation and the loneliness. One September day, when Ray was out harvesting, she'd cleaned out the house, took the kid and moved to Saskatoon. In the middle of harvest, no less. No one in the community could understand why a woman would do such a thing. Well, they could understand the leaving part, but in the middle of harvest? It was just bad timing. Some men never recover from something like that; Julie found she had a hard time meeting those sad grey eyes.

When they pulled up to the house, Julie scooted out of the cab.

Ray lifted the tire out of the back of the truck and rolled it over to Julie's car. He balanced it for a minute with one big hand and bent down to look at the treads. "She's looking a little worn, Julie. Hope you're not planning to take a big trip with these tires." He flopped the tire onto the driveway.

Julie shook her head. "Actually, I was just waiting for school to get out so I could get to the city and buy new ones." She wondered what it would be like to be taken care of by a man. A man would know when to change a furnace filter, when to trade the car in and how much to pay for a new one.

"Sooner rather than later would be the best, I'd advise." He looked serious.

His big hand on the door handle now. Julie'd never seen such big hands. She stared. She should have asked him in for a drink, but he was already maneuvering his long legs back into the cramped cab. He touched his cap to her and then backed out of the driveway.

She watched the truck until it turned left by the United Church and was lost to her sight.

\*\*\*

That evening Julie went walking out past the town across the railroad tracks and south along the grid road. She'd felt restless all day, as if she had a fever burning inside her. She hadn't been able to get her mind on anything, and of course it didn't help that the phone never stopped ringing: Emily Watson, organizer of the vacation bible school, begging Julie to help her out and take charge of the seven and eight year olds, Joanie Sparks from the United Church Women, asking if she could make a slice for Mrs. Connor's funeral on Tuesday next. Julie felt that the little town with all its expectations and demands was like an aggressive clematis plant, its vines and tendrils reaching out to choke her. She pushed back her shoulders, as if she could physically push the thoughts from her mind.

The hay in the ditches adjoining the town was completely cut now and the shorn grass lay at the side of the road in great uneven clumps, waiting to cure before baling. A feeling close to grieving pressed in on her. It had to do with the end of the school year, Michelle and Tanya leaving town, the visit to Sid's Garage this morning. She felt as if one part of her life was over, that things could not stay the same and that something or someone new would enter it to redefine and shape who she was.

Off to the right the sun was sliding into the horizon. Julie stood at the side of the road and looked west. Waiting. Just waiting.

## 2. *That Autumn*

Julie stood at the kitchen sink washing tomatoes for the third batch of salsa in as many days. She could see a man next door unloading his possessions from the back of a Ford half-ton. A mattress tied with binder twine like a bale of hay, a battered portable television set, and an impressive looking stereo system. She was alarmed at the size of the speakers; they were as big as dressers. He seemed to enjoy the physical exertion required by the hoisting and carrying, obviously a man who was no stranger to this kind of work. Once in a while he lifted his ball cap and wiped his brow with one motion. Julie noticed he was lean without being too thin, but he had just the beginnings of a little paunch developing under his striped cowboy shirt, nothing too serious, just a small betrayal of the body.

She felt like a voyeur. What if he suddenly spun around and caught her spying? It might make for an awkward beginning. She turned her back and began chopping tomatoes and peppers and onions, measuring in the spices and seasoning. She couldn't believe her garden this year, the bounty. Every day this fall she'd brought boxes of vegetables to school to give away to her colleagues: mounds of tomatoes, trunk loads of zucchinis, grocery bags of cucumber and squash. Recently, her neighbours turned and went the other way when she approached them on the street. One evening when she'd been out jogging she'd caught the United Church minister's wife dumping a prize zucchinni on the compost pile in her backyard. She had to smile.

Through the screen door the smells of autumn crowded in on her: the ripened grain in the fields circling the town, the gardens sensuous with produce, the decaying leaves. She noticed as well how the air had suddenly turned crisp, how the birds had quieted, were gathering together, making travel plans for the great migration. She turned from the window and looked down at her hands; she saw that they bore the brunt of this year's pickling and canning. She never could bring herself to wear rubber gloves in the kitchen. She should have learned her lesson from last year, the way the jalapeno peppers had eaten her hands and left them red and raw. She put the salsa mixture to simmer on the stove, stirring it once in a while with an oversized wooden spoon. She lined up her quart jars in a shallow baking pan, added an inch of water and set them scalding on the back burner. The sharp smell of the salsa cooking burned a path through her nostrils. A sure sign it was going to be good; maybe she'd take a jar over to the new neighbour tomorrow.

She wondered what calamity this new tenant would bring. Lately, small-town Saskatchewan had become a haven for people looking for a cheap place to live. There'd been a parade of them next door in the last few years, a guy from B.C. who tried growing marijuana in the basement until he got busted, a couple of teenaged dropouts who made the place into party central for a few months, leaving a trail of broken beer bottles up the back alley. It had taken quite a bit of trouble to get them evicted. She'd had to make her case at a town council meeting, without the support of anyone else on the street, and then had to write several letters to various government departments. She was pretty sure she didn't want the hassle of another go around.

She gave the salsa a final stir and then ladled the thick sauce into the sterilized jars. After standing them to cool on a tea towel, she looked around the kitchen at the sealers of dill and bread and butter pickles, the tomatoes and beets, the green beans. She loved the way the canned vegetables gleamed in their jars like precious jewels. She'd have to cart them down to the cold room soon, she was running out of space up here, but she liked looking at them. She had no idea what she'd do with it all. Give half of it away, she supposed.

She glanced through the kitchen window; everything was dead quiet. He must be finished moving in. She was curious about him in a detached kind of way. She supposed she'd find out sooner or later what he was doing in town. She decided she'd leave a jar of salsa on his back step with a little note stuck on top.

*** 

News travels faster than the speed of light in a small town. Julie found out the next day in the staff room who her next door neighbour was. Wayne Larson, the shop teacher, had the whole scoop; he'd been at Sid's Garage that morning getting gas.

"Julie, have you met your new neighbor yet?" he teased.

"Well, no, I haven't met him."

"Apparently, he moved in yesterday. Craig Houston's his name. He's a crop duster." Wayne took a long satisfied sip of his coffee like he was pulling on a beer. He enjoyed being the first one to know something.

Julie registered a little flicker of interest. "A crop duster?" she said blandly. "What would he be doing here now? All the crop spraying is done for this year, isn't it?" She grabbed the last of the coffee in the pot and scoped out a seat in the middle of the old boys' network. The male teachers had tried to drive her out of the staff room years ago with their lewd jokes and sexually explicit comments, but times had changed. With sexual harassment policies in place, Julie could sit in the staff room and banter with the best of them.

"Well," said Wayne, "he's probably got a job at one of the seed cleaners or that big new pig operation north of the creek." He banged his cup down on the table with some authority. "Until spring and the spraying season starts up again."

Kevin Sanders, the lanky phys. ed teacher, responded. "I wonder how long he's been crop spraying. I hear the average life expectancy of a crop duster is five years." He fingered the shiny coach's whistle he wore around his neck on a jaunty red, blue and white striped ribbon.

"They have to fly too low, you see." Although Wayne was thirty-nine-years-old and still lived at home with his mother, he spoke with the confidence of a man used to talking about things in a man's world. "There's too many hazards at that altitude. Buildings and power lines and such. And then there's no room to make a mistake. If the plane stalls, there's just not enough time to come out of it."

Julie listened, fascinated. It was hard not to be seduced by such talk. But when the buzzer sounded for the final class, her mind had already switched to the chaos of grade nine English: how was she going to cope with twenty-six adolescents who had hormones seeping out of their pores?

"Okay, listen up class." Julie lowered her voice hoping the students would lower theirs down to her level, a technique that sometimes worked.

"Josh, Trevor, and Melissa. I'm waiting for your book report; it's already two days late. I hope you have it here today."

She looked at the three with a reproving stare. Two weeks into the school year and already the pattern had been mapped out. She knew the kids who had good intentions, but just never got around to it, and the ones who just didn't give a damn. Another school year.

Trevor was a master at diffusing the situation. "Miss Dillard, you must have had a really bad day."

Julie decided to play along. "Why's that?" she asked.

"Well, it looks like you got up this morning and put your rug on." The class broke into laughter.

Julie had to smile. She glanced at what she was wearing. A homemade jacket constructed from an afghan throw. She'd thought it looked kind of funky when she'd made it.

Trying not to smile too much herself, Julie fought to regain control of the classroom. "Thanks, Trevor. Didn't know you'd become a member of the fashion police. The book report tomorrow for sure, okay?" Julie knew she was too soft, gave them too many chances, but damn it, she wasn't going to be Mrs. Hitler, no matter what the principal expected. When she quit having fun with the kids, she'd be out of teaching for sure.

*\*\*\**

On the way home from school, Julie stopped to pick up a few provisions at the Co-op. It was part of her after-school ritual. A carton of milk for her morning cereal, a jar of low-cal tomato basil salad dressing, a head of surprisingly fresh romaine lettuce and a pack of sanitary napkins. She was premenstrual, her breasts so sore if anybody as much as looked at them she thought she'd burst into tears.

She was just passing the circular toilet paper display and backtracking through fruit and vegetables when she saw him. Her crop duster neighbour, standing there holding an over-ripe mango with a puzzled expression on his face. She thought of detouring around the onions, but realized it would have been too transparent, so she made a stealthy move to cover her package of Always with the bunch of Romaine. In doing so, she accidentally collided with his cart.

"Hi," he said in a friendly way. He tossed the mango up in the air and caught it precisely. "You wouldn't know what this is, would you?"

Julie smiled. "It's a mango. Pretty exotic for these parts. It's kind of tricky to cut into. You have to know how to do it."

"Thata fact?" He tossed the mango in the air again, caught it like it was a fly ball, and then plopped it in his grocery cart.

She was going to introduce herself, but he seemed like a man on a mission. He had that kind of deliberate, single-minded focus that one brings to a task one has never done before.

Julie hurried through the checkout; she didn't want to get caught ahead of her new neighbour with her embarrassing package of Always.

***

*Danger of frost in low-lying areas tonight* the weatherman had said on the suppertime news. Julie was covering her garden with old blankets and quilts and tarps when she heard him call across the fence.

"Hey neighbour, thanks for the tomato sauce."

She rose from the cucumber patch and pivoted. "It's salsa," she said.

He was sitting on the rickety back step with the heels of his cowboy boots wedged into the dirt, drinking a beer. "Oh, it's you, mango-lady. What a surprise. Didn't know you were my next door neighbour." He saluted her with his bottle. "Craig Houston."

Julie took off her garden gloves and poked them in the back pocket of her overalls. "I'm Julie Dillard. How'd you make out with the mango?"

He laughed. The kind of laughter that came from deep in his chest somewhere, the kind that told Julie here was a man who was used to laughing at himself.

"Well, not too good, actually. By the time I had the damn thing cut up it was just a pile of mush." He laughed again.

"It was probably too ripe. I'll show you sometime how to do it." Julie leaned her elbows on the fence. She was wary; it took her a long time to warm to someone. She couldn't help seeing a little road sign in her head that said, PROCEED WITH CAUTION.

He stretched out his legs. "See you're tuckin' everything in for the night. Need a hand?"

Julie glanced behind her where her garden did indeed resemble a yard full of sleeping bodies.

"No thanks. I'm about finished."

"Suit yourself," he said. He seemed to be a man at home with his own company.

He had an accent that she couldn't place. "You from around here?" she asked.

"North Dakota. I'm a crop duster. Heard they were short of them up here. I'll stay for a season and then move on." He pulled slowly on his beer.

"Umm." She looked down at her reddened hands and then shoved them behind her.

"I'll try and get me a job at one of the seed cleaning plants. That should hold me over until the spraying season gets going again. Can I get you a beer? You guys make good beer I havta admit." He saluted her again.

Julie didn't know if he was paying homage to her or Canadian beer in general. She guessed it was probably the latter.

"No. Thanks anyway. I should be getting in. I've got twenty book reports to mark for tomorrow."

"You a teacher?" he asked. He had this blunt way of talking as if God had rationed him out only a few words in this lifetime.

"Yes, have been for a few years. High school English and biology and special ed." She was suddenly embarrassed at having revealed even that much of herself. She looked down at her garden running shoes and toed the edge of the grass. She said lamely, "Well, nice to meet you."

It was dusk, the light ebbing into night quickly, as it did this time of year. Julie turned and made her way across the brittle grass. It was hard to walk naturally when you knew someone was watching. What did he see? she wondered. She was glad that the semi-darkness camouflaged her appearance. She tried to walk as slowly and elegantly as she could but it was hard in her clumsy running shoes and baggy overalls. She almost tripped on one of the patio blocks, an edge sticking up, but caught herself just in time by grabbing onto the stair railing. "Oh shit," she muttered and banged the screen door behind her. Did she just imagine a low chuckle coming from the other side of the fence?

***

It was after midnight when Julie finally surrendered to sleep. She'd read the Thursday *StarPhoenix* and an Alice Munro story from *The New Yorker*. She was still trying to figure out exactly what it was about and had given up. Ah, sleep. She'd had a bad case of insomnia lately. She was sure she was too young to be menopausal; there must be some other tension in her life not letting her relax. Dr. Livingston, the family doctor she'd had since she was a child, had tried to walk her through what could be the problem, but it remained a mystery.

Julie was just crossing that wonderful hazy line between drowsiness and sleep when she was jolted awake by the sound of deep bass percussion, not really music, per se, just a muffled pounding that seemed to be coming from her own basement. She sat up in bed and tried to focus. What on earth? Surely the next-door neighbour had more sense than that. He appeared to be on the edge of middle age. Old enough to know better, but then she recalled the monster speakers.

Better check it out, though, before she made any hasty judgments. Maybe one of her students had parked behind the garage and turned his stereo on just to hassle her. She groped for her Birkenstocks beside the bed, slipped her feet in and shuffled through the house, peering through all the windows. She couldn't see a soul. Damn it. It's him. She knew he seemed too good to be true. She waited. How was she going to handle this one? The neighbour on the other side of the crop duster was deaf old Mrs. Petrie. Sadly, there'd be no help coming from that quarter. She'd have to handle it herself.

So, was she going to sit here fuming all night? Was she going to go over there and bitch? Calling the cops wasn't an option; the nearest RCMP detachment was Swift Current, forty miles away. She thought she might have a pair of earplugs in the medicine chest in the bathroom. She poked around until she finally found them, wedged between a bottle of nasal spray and a tube of sunscreen. She jammed them in her ears, killed the lights, and collapsed on the bed. She knew she'd feel like a piece of string tomorrow. Remembered it was Friday, too, and the kids were always wired. Here we go again, she thought.

*** 

The crop duster disappeared for about a week after that. Lucky for him. Julie had rehearsed a million times what she was going to say to tell him off. But the days had been busy, full of exams to mark, parents to placate, problem kids pushing her patience to the limit. Truth to tell, she'd almost forgotten about the cowboy next door by the end of the week.

On Friday night, Julie had a couple of beer with the teachers after school, came home, ate a micowaved pizza, and then crashed on the couch. She watched Peter Mansbridge read the late night news without really hearing anything he said. Was she just imagining it, or was her favorite news anchor getting a tad old? She was planning her day tomorrow; she'd have to start the big garden clean up. Pull out the tomato plants and cucumber vines, uproot the corn. It was a big job. She wished now she hadn't been so ambitious in the spring when she'd planted the garden. But at the time it had been what she needed.

*Prime Minister Chretien has just returned from an African summit where he urged the nations of the western world to increase financial aid to poverty stricken African nations.* Julie thought of her cold room, a cornucopia of canned and pickled fruits and vegetables, and mused that she could probably feed a couple of African villages just from what she'd put up herself this year.

Suddenly, just under Peter Mansbridge's bland, distant voice, Julie heard a steady, primitive beat that threatened to undermine the newscast. Boom. Boom. Boom.

"Damn it." Julie tossed off the afghan, padded out to the kitchen window and peered through. Just as she thought; he was back. His half-ton parked in the backyard at a wild angle.

She'd have it out with him right now, she decided. Stupid, arrogant American cowboy. She shoved her feet in her old gardening runners, slammed the door behind her, and stomped her way through knee high grass and weeds to his back door. She took a deep breath, squared her shoulders, and then knocked three times. She was just going to bang again when he opened the door. He was wearing the same orange and teal blue cowboy shirt from a week ago, drinking a bottle of Canadian. What else? Maybe he'd just moved to Canada for the beer.

"Well, well, well. If it isn't mango-lady. Come on in." He stepped aside and made an elaborate sweeping gesture as if he was ushering her into a stylish penthouse apartment.

"No . . . no thanks," Julie stammered. She rested her fists on her hips. "Look, you're going to have to de-escalate the volume on your stereo. My windows are vibrating." Jesus, why

did she say it like that? She sounded like some prissy schoolteacher showing off her vocabulary.

"Oh Christ, I shoulda known better. Hey, just stay right
there a minute while I go do some de-escalating." He grinned.

Julie pulled her sweater down over her hips in a nervous
kind of gesture. She was starting to feel a little foolish. Maybe
she should chill out. Maybe dealing with the grade nine class
from hell was turning her into this anxious old school marm.

Still clutching his bottle of beer like a prop, Craig leisurely
picked his way through a forest of boxes back to where Julie
was waiting at the back door. Obviously, he hadn't unpacked
yet.

"I'm awful sorry 'bout that. Must be pretty thin walls on
this old shanty. Hey, can I get you a beer?" he offered.

"No, no thanks. Really. Beer gives me a headache" (This
wasn't true. She'd had two or three after school; she couldn't
remember now the exact tally). "Well, I think I'll be going.
Good-night." She backed out of the doorway.

"Adios." He saluted her with his beer.

Julie would love to have wiped the silly grin off his face.
Stupid, arrogant, unaware American, she thought.

***

The next morning Julie started gathering up the old vines and
plants that had been stripped of their produce. Tomato plants
the size of small bushes, vines of cucumber and squash that
would be the envy of *Jack in the Beanstalk*, cornstalks as tall as
Wayne Larson, the phys. ed teacher. How quickly the growing
season passed here, like a short romantic love affair, burning
itself out by the very intensity its fire created. The tomato

plants and cucumber uprooted easily, but the corn, even with its short root system was a bugger. After trying to pull them out by hand, Julie finally realized it was useless, and changed tactics. She went to get the garden spade from the side of the shed. As she rounded the corner, she momentarily gave a start. There was Craig Houston, sitting in his backyard, slouched in a lawn chair, with his feet on another one opposite. His ball cap was pulled over his face to shield it from the sun. She resisted the impulse to throw a rotten tomato at him.

Spade in hand, Julie shoved it into the hard earth, pulled back on the handle, and uprooted the dried corn stalks. She found this kind of physical work intensely satisfying. It was something to fill up the emptiness that she was losing herself in. She had just finished the first row with three more to go when Craig appeared out of nowhere. Without asking, he started piling the dead stalks into the wheelbarrow. Julie didn't know what to say. She supposed he was trying to make up for last night in his own misguided way.

She continued excavating corn stalks, one after the other, slowly and relentlessly, ignoring him. She tried not to grunt and sigh like she usually did when she was hard at something. She even began to sing a little tune. She felt just a slight edge of moral superiority, a certain lightness. They continued like this for another ten minutes, each pretending the other did not exist. In the end, it was Craig who broke the silence.

"Where would you like me to put these?" He had a wheelbarrow full of stalks and vines and half-dead tomato plants.

"Just dump them in the composter behind the garage."

She watched as he steered the wheelbarrow towards the back of the yard and tipped the contents out easily. In no time he was back picking up cornstalks and putting them in the wheelbarrow. Julie bent to her task again; he was going to catch up to her soon.

After another half-hour of serious work, Craig ventured another comment. "Gosh, woman, you sure do have a big garden. You tryin' to get the 'mother earth' award or something?"

"No, I just like gardening and putting up preserves."

"Any idea why they call it putting up? I've never heard that expression before."

"I can't imagine why they call it that. When we lived on the farm, my mum did a lot of canning and preserving. It seemed like the thing to do on the hottest day of late summer."

"So, you tryin' out for the prairie martyr award, too?" he asked.

"I don't do it because I have to, I do it because I want to. It makes all the difference."

They were getting down to the last of it now. Julie shrugged off her work shirt. Underneath, she was wearing the bright orange T-shirt her sister had given her for her fortieth birthday, a tank top with white blocky letters that spelled *Goddess in Charge*. Craig noticed it right away.

He grinned. "I agree with at least part of that statement."

Julie knew better than to ask which part. "Can I make you a cup of coffee?" she offered. "It's a little early for beer. And besides I don't drink Canadian."

In the tiny kitchen filled to overflowing with a creative mix of pottery, plants and antiques from her grandparents' farm, Julie scooped the week's collection of newspapers from a kitchen chair.

"Have a seat," she said.

She'd felt shy as if this man had invaded some private, hidden place. She busied herself at the kitchen counter measuring out coffee. How many scoops did it take? She couldn't remember, but three sounded like a fair guess. Had it been that long since she'd made a pot of coffee?

"So," she said, in an unnaturally bright voice, "tell me how you got into crop dusting. It's kind of dangerous isn't it?"

"So is living next door to a goddess."

Julie laughed. "Seriously, how long have you been crop dusting?"

Craig paused. "Four years."

His answer hung in the air creating its own space. Julie remembered the staff room conversation about the life expectancy of a crop duster being five years. She didn't let on she knew.

He continued. "We all know we're going to buy the farm someday. It just goes with the territory."

Julie figured Craig had to say that, but in his heart he thought he'd be able to defy the law of averages.

He hung onto his cup with his thumb and middle finger, ignoring the handle. He had long, flexible fingers. Her dad used to drink from a mug like that, too. Julie wondered what personality quirk that little mannerism revealed. She supposed just a lack of convention, a tendency to make things up as you went along.

Julie's kitchen was as small as a confessional; when she went to fetch the coffee pot to refill their cups, she accidentally grazed his arm that was draped over the back of his chair. His arm where he'd rolled up his shirtsleeve was tanned and blanketed with fine golden hairs and sprinkled with freckles thick as stars.

Craig didn't miss a beat. He kept on talking, telling her about being in the air force, being a commercial pilot, and then flying all over the world in his own plane. He'd been everywhere: Africa, Australia, the Arctic. She felt hopelessly untravelled and tongue-tied. One part of her wished he'd leave so she could go back to her safe little life where nothing happened and there were no expectations.

As if he could read her thoughts, Craig brought his cowboy boots down on the floor with a thud. He slapped his knees and stood up. "Thanks for the coffee, neighbour. Sorry about the noise the other night. You know, when you live alone for so long, you kind of forget your manners." His eyes swept her face and then moved down to her T-shirt. Julie stood up and walked him to the door. "Thanks for helping in the garden," she said.

"No problem," he said.

No, she thought wryly, that was probably his personal motto.

\*\*\*

Julie felt a cold front coming on; she'd added another blanket to her bed. In the mornings the hum of the furnace seduced her into wakefulness. The great bird migration had begun. At times the sky was stitched black with flocks of geese and their small town had been invaded by American hunters. Craig had been busy entertaining his friends for weeks, driving them around the countryside, staking out the best spots for the early morning fly-past. Recently, the switch from grain to pulse crops like peas and lentils had been a boon for the goose population. When harvest was over, they loved scouring the fields for leftovers.

She hadn't seen Craig for weeks, just the odd clandestine sighting early in the morning when she'd spotted him heading out with his buddies, and in the evenings sometimes, they'd sit out in the backyard and have a few beer. One morning she found a row of empties lined up on the railing of her fence, with the letters of the alphabet inscribed on the labels with red marker and a note, "Sorry, teach, we could only make it to "J" tonight." What a bunch of comics, Julie thought. Must be nice when all you have to do is think of clever ways to harass your next-door neighbour.

It was Saturday. Julie was curled up in bed, refusing to let go of a deep, disorienting sleep that almost felt drug-induced. She was hovering on the lip of wakefulness, when a loud banging at the door tunneled through her sleep. She sat up quickly like a guilty child, caught in mischief. Twisted her head to check the time. Damn it. Ten o'clock. She grabbed a fleecy housecoat and padded out to the kitchen.

She pushed her hair into some kind of order with her fingers and rubbed sleep particles from her eyes. Then flung open the door. Craig Houston was standing on the back step. He was wearing a worn jean jacket over his cowboy shirt and had taken off his ball cap. It was probably the first time she'd seen him without one. His hair was the colour of binder twine and about the same texture. She had an almost uncontrollable desire to run her hands through it. It would be the kind of hair that tangled easily.

"Oh . . . didn't expect you." She held the neck of her housecoat close together.

Craig shoved his hands deep into the back of his blue jeans. She couldn't read his eyes. "I've been meaning to ask you for a long time now. I've been wanting to see the sunken hill and the sand castle south of Beechy. The guys down at Sid's Garage were telling me about it." He leaned into the doorway. "It's a nice day. Thought maybe you'd like to ride along and show me the way. How about it?"

"Oh," she said. She could feel her pulse beating erratically on her neck where she was clutching the lapels of her housecoat together, like a drowning woman grasping for deliverance. The only sensible thing would have been to shut the door and walk away but she found herself saying, "Sure, what time did you want to leave? I've got a few chores to do around here first. How about after lunch?"

"Sounds good to me. Pick you up about one." She watched his tall spare body vault the four-foot fence dividing their lots. She smiled. Was he showing off?

*** 

They took the highway south of town, a narrow pothole infested strip of highway that should have been condemned. Unfortunately, it was the only route out for a lot of southerners. And now that most birds had been exiled to warmer climes, combines and swathers had been wintered in sheds, the land seemed bare and spiritless.

Julie sank into the rich leather seat of the half-ton and tried to relax. She couldn't take her eyes from the fretwork of fine wrinkles on his face, his long-fingered, intelligent looking hands. Julie believed that hands had their own kind of genius. Her father had hands like that, too, the kind of hands that knew their way around all manner of machinery. Craig would use his hands to manipulate his airplane, its speed and altitude, keep it flying with just the slightest twist of the wrist or pressure of the fingers.

They crested the hill, coming down into Beechy, a small town on the edge of nothing. Craig drew in his breath. Julie laughed. "I was hoping you'd do that. Most everyone does." Beyond the town, the bleached fields and pastures stretched out, reaching to the horizon.

"Man, this is beautiful country. I had no idea," he said.

"No, most people don't." Julie felt a sense of pride in this place, seemingly forgotten by the world.

They slowed to pass through the town, and then continued on past the Perrin Ranch and the Hutterite colony.

Julie directed him to turn left into an old pasture that would take them to the site. Craig navigated several washouts on the way; there'd been a recent heavy rainfall. His shiny half-ton was certainly getting initiated.

"You sure we're going to get through here?" Craig suddenly seemed unsure of himself.

"Don't worry about it, the soil's sandy here. You're not going to get stuck."

At every washout they drove through, the muddy water completely covered the truck. It would need to be hosed down when they got back to town. Finally, after several more washouts, they stopped close to the site and walked the rest of the way in.

The view of the South Saskatchewan was stunning; the river bracketed by soft brown camel-backed hills, and immediately below them the giant, naturally formed sand castle. They stared for a long time at the gorgeous view; words seemed useless. Then he said, "Come on, let's walk down to the bottom." He held out his hand and started down, leading the way. His hand was warm and sure: Julie felt a sensation like an electrical current pulse all the way to the soles of her feet. At the foot of the castle, they stood and looked up at the spires carved from the hard cracked sand; its beauty so totally unexpected.

"You okay?" asked Craig. He seemed out of breath.

"Yeah, I'm fine." Julie was breathing fast, too, but she didn't think it was from the climb. They sat down together on a small wedge of rock, their bodies barely touching. Julie watched a small speck of a motorboat put-putting its way through the swath of dense blue water. It seemed to be hardly moving. Some die-hard fisherman probably out for a final expedition before freeze-up. She watched until it disappeared behind the hills. Craig peered through his binoculars, scanning the length of the river. A V-formation of Canada Geese flew into their line of sight, heading south.

"Look," said Julie. "You didn't get them all."

He chuckled. "I hope not." He continued peering through the binoculars and then lowered them to his lap. He looked around as if he was trying to memorize the view

He let his breath out slowly. "Well," he said, "maybe we should be getting back."

"Sure. Whenever."

He pulled her up to her feet.

They had just started up the trail, when suddenly Julie felt his arms encircling her. She almost tripped and fell, but he caught her by the elbow and spun her around to face him. "Come here," he said. His arms encircled her ribs like a cage. His mouth on hers was warm and wet and demanding, his hands searching under her shirt. Julie fought to escape the sensations washing over her body, sensations she'd long forgotten. She must have had a surprised look on her face because he drew back and said, "Christ, I'm sorry. I didn't mean to . . . you know. Rush you." He turned and led the way back up. Julie wiped her mouth with the heel of her hand and followed.

Back at the truck, Craig stood with his back to her, leaning on the hood, resting on his elbows. She came up behind him and circled his waist with her long arms. "Umm . . . that feels good," she said. He had come prepared: he spread out a blanket on the prairie grass beside the truck and they undressed each other slowly. He undid the tiny buttons of her shirt, counting each one. She helped him out of his denim jacket and shirt and then tasted the salt of his skin and smelled the wind and sun and sage everywhere on his body. She desired him against all reason, and he fulfilled her hope until she gasped and cried out. Afterwards, he picked dried prairie grass from her hair, and she wrapped the too-small blanket around them against the October chill. Overhead, a hawk made a brilliant fly-past, as beautiful as a crop duster. She didn't think of the future, but only this moment, the warmth of his body, the touch of his skin, memorizing it for the day when only emptiness would fill her.

# Where We Belong

"You're the one who wants to go, not me," Neville said to Florence as they sat at the kitchen table, each with their second cup of decaff. He hated weddings and an invitation to one was always a source of argument.

"Now hush," she told him. "Going where we do not wish to go may lead us to where we belong."

"Where'd you hear that?" he snorted. "Did you make that up yourself?"

"No," said Florence. "I saw it on a little plaque at Johnson's Gift Shop the other day and I thought it made sense. It's mine now. I like it and I'm going to use it."

"You can't just steal someone else's words like that."

"Why can't I? What's going to happen to me? Will I be sent to copyright hell?"

She laughed.

Florence had him buffaloed this time. He had no answer. "What do you want me to wear to the wedding?" he asked. "I don't want to change a half dozen times because I didn't put the right thing on. Just lay my clothes on the bed and that's what I'll wear." He sugared his coffee in a haphazard way, sprinkling the table nearly as well as the cup of coffee.

Florence sighed. She looked across the table at her husband of forty-seven years and wondered how they'd arrived at this point. A swath of light shone through the east window forming a glow around Neville's head. He was tall and loose-boned with a huge shock of wiry grey hair that had not receded one bit in his seventy-one-odd years, his hairline as straight and definite as if a draftsman had drawn it there. His hair was combed directly back, but was puffed up at the top on either side so that it gave his head a strange owl-like appearance.

She rose from the table, wobbling slightly, and began to stack plates and cups in the dishwasher, her favorite household appliance. She could abide any household chore, dusting and vacuuming and scouring the bathroom, but washing dishes seemed like an endless chore and so when they'd moved into town two years ago, she'd insisted on buying a dishwasher. However, she had to admit that she'd had some of her best conversations with Neville when he used to dry the dishes. There was something about the routine that encouraged intimacy, honesty, forthrightness. She bent to her task and continued stacking.

Neville's clothes. That was another problem. She didn't know why she had to dress the man. Wasn't that a life skill you should have learned early on in life? She guessed it was Neville's strategy to wear her down about going to the wedding. Hoping she'd throw her hands up in despair and forget the whole idea.

After breakfast, Florence went into the bedroom and looked through Neville's wardrobe. Even though it was September, it was going to be a hot sluggish day, and she knew Neville would put up a fight about wearing a suit. Besides, the only decent suit he owned was a dark navy wool pinstripe. Why give him something else to complain about? There was another reason why Neville shouldn't wear the suit today. The last time Neville had worn it, he had cried like a baby. Could it really be two summers ago since Jack had died? Their darling Jack. Forty-two-years-old. The illness had come out of nowhere — some rare viral thing. Violent, swift and deadly. The anniversary of his death was next week and as the day grew closer, Florence could feel Neville's edginess growing. She had decided that going to the wedding would be a good thing. Weddings were all about new beginnings, and faith, and hope. Getting on with life.

She settled on a pair of lightweight gray flannels and a mauve shirt. She'd hear about the colour of the shirt, no doubt. Mauve was just a little suspect, seeing as how it was related to pink, according to Neville.

After she was through setting out Neville's clothes, she searched the closet for something she could wear. She slid the hangers along the rod, ruling out this outfit or that. The navy suit (too dark and sad looking), the brightly flowered shift (too Hawaiian), the peach colored shirt-waist (too secretarial). Finally, at the very end of the line she came across a dress she'd almost forgotten she had. She pulled it out and held it up to the light. A beautiful abstract print with delicate splotches of colour almost like a prairie meadow in mid-July. What had been the occasion? She never just bought a dress for the pleasure of buying a dress. Who could afford that? Then, she remembered. Jack and Francine's wedding ten years ago. How could she have forgotten? She stroked the silky fabric. That was probably the last time she had danced with her son. Like his Dad, Jack had been a good dancer, had easily moved her around the hardwood dance floor, winding his way among the other couples. And Florence had put back her head and laughed with the sheer joy of sharing this moment with her son.

She laid the dress on the bed beside Neville's clothes. If she could fit into it, that's what she would wear.

*** 

As they drove through the countryside, she could see that summer was being taken from them on all sides: the yellowing fields, the golden-red leaves on the shelterbelts, the shabby grass in the ditches. She usually drove now when they went to the city so Neville could look around at the fields that he loved. Fields that he used to work himself, and would still be working if Jack hadn't died. All the way to the city, the combines were out in full force surrounded by thick clouds of dust as they moved up and down the fields. She could smell the grain dust in the air even with all the windows closed. She glanced over at Neville knowing that he still had grain dust in his veins even though he'd retired from the farm two years ago this fall.

"It's a damn poor time for a wedding, if you ask me." Neville moved his head from side to side trying to take it all in.

"Well, Bob and Eunice are city folk now. Harvest time means nothing to them." They were neighbours who had moved to the city when farming hadn't worked out. Bob had gone into insurance. Their youngest son was getting married today.

"They should know better, just the same," said Neville.

"It's a different world out there, dear. And we're not the centre of it anymore." She drove with a confidence born of driving every kind of vehicle imaginable: the three-ton grain truck, the unpredictable half-ton with the stubborn clutch, the tractor that steered like an old wheelbarrow.

"You're over-steering Florence. You know, you're not driving the old Massey. Quit sawing back and forth with your hands. You don't hardly have to steer this car at all. It just about drives itself."

Florence ignored him. She turned the radio up a fraction. Shania was singing "That Don't Impress Me Much." Neville liked Shania.

"You gonna let that trucker stick to your bumper like that? Move on over, woman and let'm by. He'd just as soon run you down as let you live. Damn truckers. Think they own the road." He made an obscene gesture at the offending driver as Florence pulled over to the shoulder.

She hoped the trucker hadn't noticed. The words "road rage" came to mind. She waved and smiled as he roared past.

Neville beat time to Shania, his fingers clicking on the dash. It was aggravating. Florence kept her mouth shut, though. She didn't want to start anything. They were on their way to a wedding, a happy occasion. Supposedly. At least they all started out that way.

"You know, Florence, you might just as well keep up with the traffic as try to stay with the speed limit. You're just a hazard on the road."

Florence lowered her foot on the gas pedal until they were clocking a hundred and twenty clicks. They drove an older model Chevy; speed was no problem. She turned up Shania.

Suddenly, as they climbed to the crest of a short rise, Florence saw to her horror a police car coming towards them. She quickly slowed down and checked her rear-view mirror to see if it was turning around. Sure enough, the brakes went on and in no time flat, the police car was behind them, its blue and red lights signaling them to stop.

"Goddamn it," Neville said. "I knew we shouldn't be going to this wedding. Shoulda stayed home."

Florence gave him a ferocious look. "Let me take care of this. Just be quiet for a change. Hand me the registration out of the glove box."

She rolled the window down. A heavyset officer with greying hair poked his head in and said cheerfully, "Good afternoon, ma'am. Could I see your registration and driver's license, please?" He looked benignly in Florence's direction. "Did you realize, ma'am, that you were travellin' a hundred and twenty kilometers an hour? You do know what the speed limit is on this road, don't you?"

Before Florence could answer, Neville piped up. "You know officer, if you don't keep up to the traffic on this here highway, those big truckers have their noses stuck up your ass as far as they can get it."

Florence had seen this coming. She searched her brain for some form of damage control. But before she could come up with anything, Neville stormed ahead. "I don't know where you guys are when a fella needs you. A few years ago we had our windmill stolen right under our noses, and then some hitchhikers walked right into our field and stole the bloody half-ton with all our tools in it, for Christ's sake."

"Well, I'm sorry to hear that, sir. You married to this woman here?" asked the officer.

"Of course, I'm married to her," Neville snorted. "What do you take me for, anyway?"

Florence gave him a wicked elbow in the ribs. "Be nice," she said under her breath in a threatening kind of way.

The officer didn't appear upset about Neville's remarks. He looked at Florence. "Just wait here for a minute, ma'am." He took their registration and license back to the patrol car with him. A young female officer waited in the passenger's seat.

"Probably showing off for the young intern," snorted Neville.

"Neville," warned Florence, "you say anything else to get us in more trouble and you're gonna walk to the wedding."

"Ump . . . didn't wanta come, anyway."

Florence and Neville sat in the car for a long time waiting for the officer to come back. Several huge semis roared past them. They had to be going over the speed limit. Why didn't the officer stop them? Florence wondered.

"Maybe he'll decide to give us a break," Florence said.

"Don't count on it," said Neville.

After a while, the officer came back carrying some official looking papers. Florence rolled the window down. He handed her the papers. "I'm afraid I'm going to have to charge you with exceeding the speed limit."

Neville exploded. "Christ, have you got nothing better to do than harass an old couple on their way to a wedding?"

"Well, that's what you pay me for," said the officer. "To enforce the law."

"We sure as hell don't pay you to do this."

Florence rolled the window up before Neville could come up with any more rude comments.

Neville looked at the light blue paper the cop had handed to Florence. "One hundred and two dollars. Well, I'm not payin' it. I'm gonna fight it in court."

Sure you are, thought Florence. She knew Neville would eventually pay it, but not before the entire world heard about the injustice of it all.

She pulled back onto the highway, checked the time. Forty-five minutes until they had to be there. She set the cruise control at the speed limit.

***

Neville crumpled the blue paper into a ball and threw it to the floor of the car. The angry words he'd just spoken formed a hard knot in his throat. Suddenly, he felt like crying. He caught a glimpse of his face in the side mirror — an old man who looked puzzled and afraid. He looked away quickly into the field they were passing, a beautiful field of wheat that was being swathed.

"Look at the size of that swath," he said as he wiped the corners of his eyes. "It's gonna be a bumper."

His voice sounded trembly and uncertain. He looked over at Florence but she had her eyes locked on the road. Up ahead was an old abandoned farmhouse sitting in the middle of an unkempt yard, bordered by scruffy caraganas. Every time they went by it, the house seemed to sink farther into the earth. The windows were dark gaping holes.

They passed by a combine stopped at the edge of a field. An older man dressed in coveralls and a baseball cap stood talking to a younger man dressed in a red T-shirt and blue jeans. They looked like they could be father and son. Neville thumped his fist into the palm of his other hand. He felt the sting of tears start up behind his eyes and the choking emotion rise to the surface. Damn it, he thought. He thumped his fist harder. Florence looked straight ahead.

They slowed for Delisle, a pretty little prairie town with a happy mixture of small businesses and houses flanking the highway on one side, the sprawling Pool elevator on the other, and the green water tower resembling an upside down exclamation mark smack in the middle of town.

"Don't forget to stop for gas here on the way home." Neville motioned to the Co-op Service Station on the left. "It's always cheaper."

"Well," said Florence, "don't forget to remind me."

They pulled away from the town, the highway a grey passageway winding its way through a combination of farmland and park, the fields here not rectangles or squares but irregular shapes curving around bluffs of trees and pastures. Neville didn't know how they could farm here. It made him feel anxious. He preferred the fields back home — four ninety-degree corners, and straight lines. Predictable. Orderly. You knew what you were up against — no surprises.

How he envied Florence; she could handle surprises. And life had handed her a few. A stillborn child, two miscarriages, a mastectomy at forty-five. They'd both cried and then she took a deep breath and got on with it. And Jack's death. Sure, life had stopped for a few months for her, too, but then she'd got back on track. Neville felt like he'd been derailed. Permanently. He sighed.

That last harvest with Jack, Neville had operated the combine while Jack drove the truck — an arrangement that suited them both fine. Florence had brought supper to the field that night, stew and homemade dumplings. A picnic in the field. Jack's wife and the two kids had come, too, the grandchildren, Kate and Sean. They'd taken turns riding in the combine with him. Eight-year-old Sean had even taken the wheel and drove it himself for a round or two. Neville could see he was going to be a farmer one day; he could sense the desire in the boy. It had been a beautiful day, much like today, he thought. Just enough wind to keep the grain dust away, a few soft clouds scudding across a deep blue sky, the temperature of the air the same as his own skin so that he somehow felt weightless. Everything had seemed possible that day. He had dared to cast an eye into the future and he had a vision of his own grandchildren farming the land that his grandfather had broken and plowed. A continuous line like stitches on a quilt. But now the line had been severed.

They crossed the overpass and then he saw the city bunched up on the horizon. Neville was always surprised by the way it seemed to appear out of nowhere, as if in a dream.

"What time is it?" Florence said. She hadn't spoken for miles.

"It's a quarter to five. I guess we still have time to make it unless we get lost." He felt bad he'd been so grumpy with Florence back there.

"Oh, we shouldn't get lost," said Florence. "The wedding's not in a church. It's in the Bessborough, downtown."

"Christ," said Neville. "Not even gettin' married in a church. What's the matter with young people these days?"

"I guess their ways are not our ways," she said.

The city seemed strangely quiet for a Saturday. Traffic was sparse and they saw only one pedestrian walking up Twenty-second Street, a Native kid with baggy pants who walked with his head down, kicking the clumps of poplar leaves that littered the street. He looked as though he didn't have enough energy to kick a ball up the street. Neville wondered what his own grandchildren would be doing today. Sean and Kate. When Jack had died, Francine had left the farm almost immediately. Went out to Alberta where she was offered a good job as a physiotherapist. Neville could hardly blame her. Of course, she had to make a living now. But, living in Calgary? He had visions of his grandchildren walking up the street looking like refugees. He wiped his hand over his eyes as if to erase the picture.

Florence made a right turn and then a left onto Twenty-first Street. Up ahead, the Bessborough stood guard over the South Saskatchewan River. It was pretty as a picture. Neville wasn't sure, but he thought they might have spent their honeymoon there. Asking Florence was out of the question, though; there were some things a guy shouldn't forget.

They just had time to park the car and find their way to the Adam Ballroom in the big old hotel before the wedding ceremony started. The place was packed: a happy mixture of the old, middle-aged, young marrieds and their kids. Florence and Neville secured the very last two seats in the back row for themselves. It was at that moment that Neville looked over at Florence and noticed the dress she was wearing, a funny kind of printed thing. Just splotches of colour. He thought it was sort of pretty. Something about it tugged at his memory; he wished that he paid more attention to such things. He ignored the buzz going on around him and looked at Florence again. He saw a full-bodied woman with a head of curls the colour of winter and eyes the fragile blue of a flax field in full bloom. He felt like reaching over and taking her hand in his, but she was rummaging in her purse for Kleenex, getting ready for the big cry, he supposed. She always cried at weddings.

Suddenly, hand bells began to ring. On cue, the wedding guests stood and turned as one, as if they had rehearsed this moment. Neville and Florence caught sight of the bell ringers, a group of children announcing their own innocence and the wedding party at the same time. A long line of bridesmaids outfitted in cookie-cutter dresses of startling pink proceeded up the aisle followed by the shy flower girl and the reluctant ring bearer in a too-stiff white cotton shirt and prim bow tie. The bride and groom looked like something off the top of a wedding cake. Obviously, the couple had written their own vows; he was not surprised that the words honour and obey never passed their lips. A very bad soloist, accompanied by a karaoke machine, sang some country and western tearjerker that Neville didn't recognize. He drifted off for a moment; thought how life had a way of just rolling on whether you wanted it to or not. When he looked up again the bride and groom were kissing. Neville was relieved the ceremony would soon be over. He glanced to the side. Florence's face was wet with tears. He followed her gaze to the front of the room where the bride and groom were turning to face the guests. They slowly came into Neville's focus like a Polaroid picture developing. It looked trite and orchestrated, but at the same time innocent and hopeful. He reached for Florence's hand as if fumbling to find his way home.

***

Later, they danced. Florence moved so easily into his arms, that place of comfort and trust. They smiled and touched their heads together, gently. Their eyes lit up. They had borne illness and loss and disappointment over the years, but they had kept faith with each other. Time tumbled away, the picture of their grey hair and sagging bodies faded, until they almost seemed young again. Beneath the melody, Florence's words from that morning floated like counterpoint.